Water Street

Water Street

Crystal Wilkinson

Foreword by Jacinda Townsend

Afterword by Marianne Worthington

This edition made possible under a license arrangement originating with Amazon Publishing, www.apub.com.

Printed in the United States of America.

2017 edition published by the University Press of Kentucky, scholarly publisher for the Commonwealth, serving Bellarmine University, Berea College, Centre College of Kentucky, Eastern Kentucky University, The Filson Historical Society, Georgetown College, Kentucky Historical Society, Kentucky State University, Morehead State University, Murray State University, Northern Kentucky University, Transylvania University, University of Kentucky, University of Louisville, and Western Kentucky University.

Editorial and Sales Offices: The University Press of Kentucky
663 South Limestone Street, Lexington, Kentucky 40508-4008
www.kentuckypress.com

The story "My Girl Mona" was previously published in *The Indiana Review* and was the winner of the 2001 Indiana Review Fiction Prize

Cataloging-in-Publication data is available from the Library of Congress.
ISBN 978-0-8131-6910-1 (pbk. : alk. paper)

This book is printed on acid-free paper meeting the requirements of the American National Standard for Permanence in Paper for Printed Library Materials.

Member of the Association of American University Presses

For Stanford, Kentucky, and long, wonderful summers

Contents

Foreword

Jacinda Townsend

I discovered Crystal Wilkinson's words halfway through my first year of graduate school. Like many first-year MFA students, I was still so unsure about the choice I'd made just six months prior; I'd given up a career in New York and moved halfway across the country for a chance at two years of writing and learning, but belonging to an MFA program had not, for me, translated into a sense of *belonging*. I found precious little community in my program. These were the days before cell phones and unlimited calling plans; I missed my boyfriend. I missed seeing live jazz on the weekends. And money was tight. *Tight.* Even as I sat typing, occasionally taking a break from the life of my imagination to watch the snow beautifully burying my little green Honda under the mythic Iowa sunset, the dream seemed to have gone all wrong.

I remember, then, as one might remember one's first time tasting Greek pastry or first time at the apex of the Navy Pier Ferris wheel, the pivotal moment of my finding Crystal Wilkinson's work.

Here was a writer not at all wed to the drudgery of canon: Wilkinson's quick wit, haunted characters, and simple yet all-encompassing voice inserted a freshness into a literary landscape that I'd come to view as painfully standard. Here was a writer giving voice to a life that I myself had lived but never seen represented—Black Kentucky, the mid-southern African diaspora, the Affrilachia that literature previously had not acknowledged. "We are almost Southern," Wilkinson writes in *Water Street*'s opening story, "but not northern at all." As a writer, I found that reading Wilkinson's work inspired me to reach back into my own culture for its many untold stories; as a reader, I discovered that her work meant even more. If, finally, this culture of mine could be communicated in this way, with language so beautifully timeless and lyrical, then so many others would come to be steeped in it, for the duration of this literary visit and beyond. At last, I too could lay claim to having been represented on the page: in the grand ballroom of literature, I could finally, as a Black Kentuckian, claim to exist.

Crystal Wilkinson has done so much as a literary citizen to draw Black Kentucky on the map of American narrative, but *Water Street* is the push tack of her delicious writing itself and of her unforgettable characters, who wind their ways from story to story, all against the backdrop of Stanford, Kentucky, which is, in the real world, one of Kentucky's oldest settlements. There's Mona, who "doesn't seem like she's from Stanford at all anymore. She has swallowed her small town twang and is speaking in some generic tone that doesn't even say Lexington." Jeanette who, when she kisses boys, is "searching for an abyss in which I could escape through."

Each story builds on the one that came before, in some cases telling from the perspective of the person just told, creating a binding dynamism that grows to encompass not only the characters but also this very special moment in history in this unique place. We first meet Yolanda as she reflects on feeling like her husband Junior's "second place trophy," and we follow the couple as well as Yolanda's brother Kiki through various points of emotional resonance, finally meeting up with them on the occasion of Yolanda's sinking into a deep depression just before her brother Kiki jilts his bride. We are, then, shown a narrative trajectory of loss, of winning, of treasure among the ruins, of rain falling against the dawning sun. In "Water Street, 1979," Junior uses his voice to make us linger with the complexity of race relations in this place, to make us sit under the uncertain mists that hang between Black and White residents of Stanford. It still resonates in a "postracial" America that nonetheless presents grave danger to its minorities.

Wilkinson achieves all this with the most lyrical description in all of American literature. "Mama has never been one for appearances," she writes in "The Fight." "There is no magic in her cleaning skills. The house is not filthy or nasty. It's just messy. Piles of paper in the corners—bills, articles torn from magazines, mimeographed copies of poems my mother liked in high school, old photographs of Grandpapa before he died, and Mama dressed in pleated, long skirts and sweaters when she was young." She writes life into the people of Stanford and its environs in "My Girl Mona," writing "her mascara-rimmed eyes are meddling with the people eating in the booths around us. Flirting with Mr. Taylor, who's stuffing a hamburger in his mouth, mustard running down his chin. Nodding hello to Callie Sumner, who owns the restaurant. . . . She saunters by with a large, orange tray filled with hamburgers and fries held high above her head, her flabby arms flopping in her own wind." A person could live three lifetimes, the reader senses, and not see the world in all the permutations that Wilkinson describes.

Jeanette, the narrator of "In Plain Sight," says, "I don't think we have a choice in the spirits who haunt us. We have to settle for what we get." And happily, this is how it was for me as a reader of Crystal Wilkinson: there, in the middle of my uncertainty as a new writer, Wilkinson inspired me with the dazzling beauty of this world she had created, and became one of the writers for whom I was writing. For I did not discover the world of *Water Street* so much as this world discovered me. It is a world made so real, in such Technicolor, that it reaches out to the reader and says *You. Come. Join me here. Water Street* is a place of inventive prose and fresh characters, and readers will feel grateful that Crystal Wilkinson has invited them to the block party.

This is a work of fiction. As a child, I spent many summers in Stanford, Kentucky, a place I considered a second home. This book is set there but the characters portrayed here and the events that take place on these pages should not be construed as real. The lives portrayed in this book are the product of my imagination.

Crystal Wilkinson

Welcome to Water Street

We are almost Southern but not northern at all. Stanford's black children root here. Some of her white ones too. This street is our homeland.

In the summer you will see our cinnamon sons, our dusty daughters wallowing in plastic swimming pools in our backyards. Girls with Chinese jump ropes fashioned from a long string of rubber bands or hula hoops swirling around their hips. Boys playing peggy bounce or kickball. You will smell the smoke from charcoal grills. Hear the chicken and the steaks sear. If you peep through the shrubs you might catch us some sweltering afternoon with our sweet iced tea glasses turned up and our bellies full of saucy baby-back ribs, collards or kale fresh from our gardens, roasted corn on the cob or homemade potato salad. We'll even share some if you like. We are that kind of people.

There are flowers in our mothers' gardens. Vegetables too. Zinnias and okra. Big boy tomatoes and yellow sunshine squash. Begonias and black-eyed susans. Sunflowers and runner beans. Potatoes and carrots, turnips and yams are rooted in our soil. Pumpkins come fall, bigger than your head.

Even in these times our mahogany and oak-cast children ride bicycles along our street. They take long walks into town to Carter's Grocery to feast on barbecue potato chips, red pop and fudgesicle bars. There you can buy a hogshead cheese sandwich for a dollar and get chopped steak and pork chops on credit if your mother sends a note.

Our children are not bad but they are accustomed to being shooed from neighboring fields. Still, somehow they always escape with an acceptable stash of green apples or juicy red tomatoes. Our teenagers lay on their backs at night and talk to each other and the stars right out in the street up on the hill. Katydid and cricket symphonies sprinkle the dark of night here. We have streetlights but we are not quite country. Not city at all.

In the winter, grandmothers quilt the way their mothers' mothers taught them to. Pots are full of homemade chili and vegetable soup made with summer's backyard bounty. Children sled and have neighborhood snowball fights. We have hot chocolate get-togethers and coffee sharing evenings in each other's living rooms.

Our men are one generation removed from farming but they still wear their farmer's clothes underneath work uniforms to remember where they're from. We still know the old folks' ways even if we keep it to ourselves. When the town trucks don't make it up here to salt our street, we are content with being snowed in, knowing we still have our fathers' fathers' ways to keep us safe and warm and fed.

Water Street is a place where mothers can turn their backs to flip a pancake or cornmeal hoecake on the stove and know our children are safe.

We are a hardworking bunch. The hawk soaring each morning in our beautiful sky sees the yellow bus that scoops up our children and takes them to school and our cars departing to factories, to beauty shops, to offices, to the neighboring towns.

We are the people who fix the streetlights, ring up the groceries or the new clothes. We keep the books straight. We nurse the sick. We sew buttons. We answer the phone. We deliver the mail. Deliver the truckloads. We keep the factories running. We type the papers. Run the office. We teach the kids.

Because there is not always work nearby some of us migrate to Danville, to Somerset, to Lexington, even Louisville. Sometimes we are on the road for hours a day, but feel at ease when we go home. It's a choice we've made because we love our clean street, pristine yards, comfortable porches. We are safe here. We are plain and we are fancy.

We love being close to the people we've known since we entered the world. And we hate it. Everybody knows your name here. Everyone has committed the long lists of your kin to memory.

We are a God-fearing people. Baptists mostly. We attend church every Sunday. Some of us still worship where our parents' parents received the Lord. But some of us have moved away and they are the ones who miss this street the most. They will always belong here even when they think they no longer do.

On Water Street, every person has at least two stories to tell. One story that the light of day shines on; the other that lives only in the pitch black of night, the kind of story carried beneath the breastbone, near the heart, for safekeeping.

My Girl Mona

Yolanda

My Girl Mona

He's short and bald, round like a black snowman but handsome. He's my head doctor, the third psychiatrist I've seen this year. The doctor leans back in his soft green leather chair and brings the tips of his fingers together like he's wise. He's not the smiley type. He nods and that's my cue to start talking.

Mona is forty-three and still got the kind of body that makes brothers act a fool, I say.

I look at Doctor like: *You know what I'm saying*? Doctor clears his throat.

We was sitting in that little diner off US-150, catching up like we do once a month, I tell him. I was sipping my 7-UP, trying not to think about how much better Mona looks than me. More kids, more husbands, but she still looks like she did in junior high. Dark skin, perky titties, a waist that curves in tight then fans out into hourglass hips for miles.

The doctor says I'm having panic attacks, I tell Mona, and I go through the rigmarole of symptoms: heart flutters, dizzy spells, the sweats, an odd feeling of otherworldliness. When I say *otherworldli-*

ness, Mona looks at me like she's being held hostage, but I keep talking. She takes a toke off her third cigarette, which takes away from her good looks. I've heard brothers say that about her, you know, wrinkling up their noses like smoking a cancer stick sends Mona from fine to ugly that quick.

You know what I mean? I say to Doctor, not as a real question but just to be saying it. He just nods like he knows.

The waitress, who is so skinny her collarbones show through her tight knit blouse, freshens Mona's coffee with a trembling hand like the pot is full of rocks. She looks at Mona with an eyebrow raised. Mona, with all her flash, is a fish out of water in Stanford now.

Mona's always been a part of my life, I say to Doctor. I still see us as little girls sometimes even now when we get together. Doesn't seem that long ago when we played down by the old creamery or recited our memorized verses in unison in front of God and everybody in the church, but it's been almost thirty years now. I was the everyday girl—not bony, not fat, not dark, not light—the girl who carried her opinions in her neck. Right here, I say to him and press my fingers into the center of my throat, a big old knot.

You were in training for panic attacks even then, Doctor says.

Doctor, she was something, I say. Mona was the one who could draw every eye across a room.

Back when everybody was trying to have that perfect Angela Davis 'fro, Mona opted for the Farrah Fawcett look even before it caught on. She had long hair for a dark sister—down past her shoulders. Mona was always trying to shellac her skin with lightener, but I loved her walnut-hull brown. She was the first black girl in Stanford to be prom queen. Mona was always first. The first to get her period, the first to sprout butt and tits, the first to "do it." If Doctor had been a light-skinned brother or a white man he would have turned red.

The summer I turned fourteen, Junior, my husband to this day, was the one boy we could tolerate. He was the kind of boy who was all-boy but could hang out with the girls without grabbing his private place. He wasn't like all them other nappy-heads who played kick ball under the streetlight. The girls would sit on the curb in our halter-tops and hot pants, trading pullout posters from *Right On!* magazine—swapping Ricky Sylvers for Michael Jackson and listening to the Ohio Players on Mona's eight track. When the game was over the boys turned their attentions to us. We all stayed out until our mamas called us home. Or until the mosquitoes started biting so hard that we all would run home itching, welts rising up all over our little hot bodies.

That year, it seemed like me and Mona spent every day of our lives wondering what it would be like to be kissed by a boy. We watched our mamas' stories on TV and read the dirty parts of every romance book we could find. We wondered what "doing it" really felt like, even though neither of us wanted the label that came with the girls who let boys touch. But we already knew there were girls like Jeanette Stokes, who actually went into one of the unlocked cars parked along the street and let a boy untie her top so he could see her breasts. And she let one of the boys she really liked finger her in the dark. The ironic thing about it, though, was that even through all that, Jeanette Stokes was still a virgin when we graduated from high school but Mona wasn't.

Doctor catches me remembering, staring off into empty space that makes up my yesterdays and then I come on back.

Through the smoke cloud, Mona strokes her red acrylic nails, extends them out like crawdad claws to pick up her knife and cuts her chicken sandwich, I continue telling Doctor. She clears her throat and fidgets with the collar of her blouse, then smoothes invisible wrinkles from her skirt. I know she can't wait for me to hush, but I keep on talking like my life depends on it.

Imagine that, I tell her. Hell, I've never had anything like this before. Junior had to take me to the emergency room the first time it happened. I thought I was having a heart attack. I've always been healthy. No, never had anything like this before. Not when cancer took Grandmama or when they fired me up at the factory. They said it was a permanent lay off. Not even when Junior messed around on me with that white woman. That bit of juice gets Mona's attention and I stop talking for just a second before I start back up, timing it just right, making sure it's not long enough for her to jump in.

Oh, I guess shit happens, I say. Guess I'm getting older. Right at that moment, as always, I'm trying to figure out on my own exactly why Mona's been my girl all these years.

And why do you think that is? Doctor asks me, leaning forward like he's getting close to an answer.

Don't know, I say to him, it's a long story.

So I can see that I am making Mona nervous, I continue telling him. I'm waiting for Mona to chime in with a friend's concern or at least to tell me how sorry she is to hear about my nervous condition but she don't. I'm waiting to hear: *What are you going to do? Is there anything I can do? Can they give you something for it?* But her mascara-rimmed eyes are meddling with the people eating in the booths around us. Flirting with Mr. Taylor, who's stuffing a hamburger in his mouth, mustard running down his chin. Nodding hello to Callie Sumner, who owns the restaurant. We went to high school with Callie. She saunters by with a large, orange tray filled with hamburgers and fries held high above her head, her flabby arms flopping in her own wind.

I guess we are all getting old. Getting fat. Mona's not even listening to me. When she looks back in my direction, I switch subjects and tell her about Junior's teaching job up at the Middle School. He is one of the first black teachers in the county.

Did you know that, Doctor?

No, I didn't. That's interesting.

I tell her about Daddy's trip to the hospital with appendicitis. I finish by telling her about my daughter, Shauna, getting caught shoplifting up in Lexington.

She's just driving us crazy, I say. We had to go up there and get a hotel for two days to get it all straightened out.

But all of these are things Mona probably already knows from the newspaper or the grapevine. Nobody's business is sacred in a small town.

I can see that I've got Doctor's full attention. He's looking at me starry-eyed like a boy listening to a tall tale.

By the end of that summer all of us girls had at least been kissed, I tell him. Even Candy Patton, the quietest and most religious among us, prayed for seven straight days not to go to hell because she let Peanut rub on her ass. It's all right, they're married now.

I should have said 'hind end' in front of Doctor but I didn't. I was comfortable, like we were old friends.

Somehow we had willed the girliness out of our bodies, I say. Instead of playing hide-and-go-seek, or hopscotch, or Chinese jump rope, or watching the boys play kick ball—in the shadows, against somebody's daddy's Plymouth or Nova, we paired up with the boys and kissed. We turned our heads to the side, puckered and kept our lips shut tight so the boys could keep their germs to themselves.

I can't help but to start laughing.

Anything else? Doctor says to me, crossing his legs in their expensive britches adjusting his self, wide in the chair, where I can see the folds of his crotch and not cracking a smile.

What do you remember most about this? Tell me everything, Doctor says and reaches over and squeezes my wrist like that's a comfort. And it sure nuff is.

Me and Mona named ourselves the kissing experts after seeing my brother, Kiki, and his girlfriend, Ina, on the couch, I say. We crouched outside the doorway of the living room, a place my mother never let us go into. The living room that was always ten times cleaner than the rest of the house, where the antiques and the good coffee table and the glass-topped lamp stood. The centerpiece was the white couch, still covered in plastic, that Daddy bought for Mama one year with the income-tax money. That living room was the show-off room only reserved for company, especially out-of-town company. It was the one thing my country mother had that rivaled anything belonging to the relatives who would ease back home from Cincinnati driving their new Cadillacs or Bonnevilles.

Kiki met Ina up at the Lexington Mall and drove his green Impala up to see her every weekend. When he brought her home to meet us, Mama told me and Mona to stay out from underfoot and let Kiki have his privacy. But me and Mona were looking through a crack in the door to the living room when Kiki and Ina kissed so much, their tongues going in and out of each others' mouths, that they looked hungry, like two starved people feasting on Christmas dinner. Me and Mona looked at each other horrified at first, but we were also looking when Kiki's hand rubbed all over Ina like mad and disappeared under her green paisley culottes. We took notes in our diaries and secured our secrets with the turn of the little gold diary keys we wore around our necks.

Now we know how it works, Mona says in a whisper, clutching her diary to her chest, her eyes fluttering up toward the ceiling like a prayer had been answered. I nodded, yes, without speaking a word. Stunned. Never believing my brother—who I deemed Big Nasty for not lifting the seat on the toilet, the one who denied me his barbecue potato chips or candy sticks, the brother who tried to coax me into washing his funky laundry—could be capable of making a girl moan and smile the way Ina did.

Later that day, Kiki walked hand-in-hand with Ina all over Stanford. Ina with her fashion-model looks and in-style clothes and Kiki with his football-player muscles were a sight to see. Everybody saw them walking down Water Street to Maxwell Street on their way to Carter's Grocery for ice cream, their perfect eight-inch Afros side by side like two black moons.

While they were gone, me and Mona pilfered Ina's purse and claimed her Satin Dreams lip-gloss for our own. We shared it as a token of our sexual orientation. In secret we slathered it on our lips and tried to cut our eyes and walk with our hips rocking the way Ina did. We even talked Kiki into driving us to the Lexington Mall one weekend so we could buy ourselves some wooden high-heeled shoes just like the ones that Ina wore with her hip hugger blue jeans.

Up until the time Kiki and Ina broke up, me and Mona would stare at her and follow her around when she was in town, hoping to get hold of some of her twenty-year-old womanly secrets.

I laugh and Doctor smiles, then catches himself and takes the smile back quick. I guess he thinks he's not being professional. I'm wishing he would just come off this for a minute and just be the black man that a sister girl needs to share her problems with and not *the doctor.*

So, anyway, I say to Doctor. I know Mona's been waiting for the conversation to open up one fraction so she can come in full force and fill it to the brim with her, so I ask her how she's doing.

Well, she says, running her fingers through her hair, then patting it down in the front and pursing her lips together to refresh her lipstick, I'm doing fine. No drama, she says.

But of course that was just warm-up talk; with Mona there's always drama. Soon Mona is smiling and gesturing wildly across the table. I listen as she sifts through child support and alimony, great sex and the kids like she's prom queen again—fake smiling so wide her unsightly dark gums show. It's an unflattering look and I catch myself relishing the snickers that Mona hasn't noticed, that are coming from the two lanky brown girls who are drinking milkshakes across from us. Look at that old lady trying to be hip, is what I'm sure they're saying. Well maybe 'hip' is not the word they use these days.

Mona doesn't seem like she's from Stanford at all anymore. She has swallowed her small town twang and is speaking in some generic tone that doesn't even say Lexington. I wonder how she could have moved only fifty miles north of here, yet be such an outlander. Her clothes are young—a bright blue blouse with enough opened buttons to show a peek of the black bra underneath, a tight black skirt that I can see only the beginnings of above the table, her legs are crossed and one of her white, girlish platform shoes is bobbing up and down into the aisle while she talks.

Doctor, Mona outgrew me in high school. I just looked up one day and she was a younger version of our mamas and I was still a girl. It wasn't her body so much, which had blossomed in junior high, but something else. She was suddenly able to hold the gaze of a man without giggling or looking away. I first saw her use it on my brother, Kiki, who was twenty-five at the time.

I stop talking.

Continue, Doctor says. Interesting, he says like I'm a bug under a microscope. And so I keep on with my story like I have to.

Mona stayed over one Saturday night in our junior year, I continue, enjoying Doctor's full attention. We had planned to stay up all night, cornrow each other's hair and try on new makeup, but Mona spent the whole night sitting in my bed, straddle-legged in her baby doll pajamas, trying to hold my brother's attention as he walked by the room. She told me she had to use the bathroom but soon I heard her in Kiki's room.

Get out of here girl, I heard Kiki say through the walls.

But soon their voices were lowered and I could hear the familiar squeaking of the bed and the grunts and snorts that Kiki made when he would sneak girls over. I expected silence from Mona. Thought she'd try to protect me from knowing, but the moaning sounds she made were so loud that I feared that my parents would come to investigate.

Later, I heard water running in the bathroom but Mona still brought the smell of sex with her into my bedroom.

Y'all out of toilet paper, she said, never saying a word about screwing my brother.

I stared at her and rolled my eyes.

What? she said.

What you think? I said.

Didn't nothing happen, she said. But I knew she was lying.

After that I think Mona hoped that Kiki would prance her around like he had Ina, but when Mona was around, Kiki would sull up and find a reason to rev up his Impala and be gone. I could tell she was hurt by it all, but she never let on. Even as close as me and Mona were, there were a million miles between us.

Keep going, Doctor says prodding out my lifeline.

A short time after that, we went to the skating rink in Danville. I watched Mona skate right over to Junior and rub his chest. Under the black lights and the strobe flashing with the music playing a slow song, Junior looked as helpless as I felt when Mona kissed him full on the lips. Junior, who was supposed to be *my* boyfriend, followed her around for weeks, lingering at my locker, talking to me, but waiting on Mona to come by. It was clear that Mona really didn't want Junior, that he was being used for target practice and looking back, I want to think that she didn't mean me any harm. That she was just testing herself, trying to grab back something lost. Junior tells me to this day that it was nothing.

I married you, didn't I? Leave the past in the past, he says.

When he messed around on me, I'd barely give him a chance to apologize before I took him back.

Doctor says I should have expressed my feelings.

Later that night, when Junior holds me in his arms, I will get tickled about that. If I had expressed my feelings, Junior would still have a skillet mark on his head.

What you laughing at? Junior will ask me and I will say, Nothing.

Ever wish you married Mona? I ask him sometimes.

Woman, he says back, we were teenagers. Ain't you ever gonna give up on that?

Then he kisses me and we make love. But even then, with him on top of me, I am less assured. Feel like I'm a second place trophy.

I slow down my story to make sure Doctor is still following me.

So when Mona says: *Darling, I have a blessed life*, like she's the Gabor sister from *Green Acres* or some other made-for-TV white woman, my heart pounds out of my chest and sweat pours down my back. My chest is closing in and I'm shaking like a leaf. I am sure that any moment somebody in the restaurant will notice my predicament and holler for Callie to call the life squad. I'm waiting for that shift of time when Mona leaves her own world for just a second and notices that I'm in trouble. But she doesn't, and all the eyes in the place are darting toward Mona. I don't say a word and just ride that one out.

Good! Doctor says, louder than I think he means to. You have to teach yourself to do that, to speak to your rational self and as you say, ride it out.

Mona's voice dims to the humming the deep freezer makes when I'm ironing clothes in the basement.

I'm not dying. I'm not dying, I say to myself over and over. It's just another spell. It's just another spell.

In a matter of minutes that seem to draw out for a lifetime, everything leaves, and then becomes clear again.

In the parking lot, after we've parted, Mona turns, waves to me and hollers, See you next time. I'll let you know about the wedding. She says and winks. There is no *I hope you feel better* or *let me know how you're doing.* I wave back and watch her heels clicking across the asphalt toward her Volvo.

I couldn't say anything I had on my mind to say, I tell Doctor.

I see, Doctor says, knocking his posed fingers against his forehead. You did well though, he says, I think you are getting better. You are gaining control. And you look so good today, he adds, well rested.

But I know he's thinking I'm screwed up in the head. He's a brother too, which makes it worse. There is so much more I want to say. So much more I want to know. I want to ask him if he's married, and if he is, whether he'd cheat on his wife. I am wondering if he would find Mona attractive. I want to ask him if he's hungry. If he wants to go get a bite to eat just to talk some more. I want to bury my head into his shoulder and just cry, but I can't, I've already told him too much. In a few minutes he will write me a prescription, shake my hand and schedule me another appointment. But before that moment he gives me a smile. A genuine smile that I snuggle in and feel clear down to my toes. And I am waiting with hope for what comes next.

Water Street, 1979

Junior

Water Street, 1979

Back then, I was growing an Afro just like every other brother in the country. We were plain old Kentucky boys but all of us had hair that stood out around our heads like halos. We were learning how to be the 'black people and proud' that James Brown summoned us to be on his record, no matter what our parents said. We wore our bellbottoms creased down the front of each leg and brought our music into the street with portable eight track tape players. I was just starting to smell my own piss and went out of my way to say what I pleased to anybody who crossed me. My wife, Yolanda, laughs when I talk about this. She says I have no room to complain about the kids today. I'm a teacher and kids are my life. But when I was a youngster, I took short cuts through white folks yards just to tee them off. Black ones too for that matter. Dared somebody to say something.

My parents didn't understand me but I think they were just as confused as I was. They warned me of the evils of white girls who ran after black boys, but Lois Carter, a redheaded white woman, was one of my mother's best girlfriends. Lois Carter came to our house to play a hand of tonk or spades and drink sweet iced tea on our porch. I heard her, right along with my mother's black girlfriends, talking about the perils of men. Sitting with her ample breasts falling from some outfit too tight for her size, she talked about her man, Roscoe.

"I told Roscoe he'd better shape up or I was shipping his black ass back home to Lancaster with his mama," I heard her say one night. "Shoot, I ain't taking his shit. Let his mama pick up his dirty drawers."

The other women laughed, their heads bobbing up and down in agreement, like she was a for-real sister. The contradiction puzzled me then. It still does.

Some of the little white girls in my classroom remind me of Lois Carter, especially Sara in my fourth-hour language arts class. If I closed my eyes and listened to Sara speak, I would swear she was black with her blonde-haired, blue-eyed self. "Girl, you betta tell him to step off before he gets a for-real ass kicking." I keep quiet, waiting for the other girls to put her in her place but they don't say anything. They slap their palms together in approval. Little blonde-haired Sara seems to fit right in. Children are amazing.

I don't know what to tell my daughter about race so I don't tell her anything. She's in high school and I don't know what I would say if she brought a white boy home. I think I would work hard on saying nothing as long as he was decent.

"Oh, Junior, hush," my mother said when I asked her about Lois Carter. "Lois? She's practically one of us. She's been around black folks her whole life."

"She's still white ain't she?" my father said, rolling his eyes.

"For shame, Walter!" Mama yelled across the kitchen, shaking her mixing spoon in Daddy's direction.

"Black folks need to stick together!" I said stepping between them. I pumped up my fist in a black power salute and tried to give them both five on the black-hand side but you know my parents weren't cool enough to follow my lead. "My people, my people," I said shaking my head in false disgust. And I pimp-walked out of the room leaving them laughing so hard they had to lean on each other to keep from falling on the floor.

My all-knowing father, who had sat me down many times to tell me about the birds, the bees and the white folks, was one of the first men to jump in the truck and drive to the edge of the flood line to help the MacIntoshes load up their furniture before it floated away. All the blacks lived at one end of Water Street above the hill, all the whites lived on the other end, where April rain sent them scurrying to higher ground.

It was a biblical rain—the forty days and forty nights type. It started out one night, soft and warm like a bath shower. The kind of rain that kids like to play in and lovers walk in. It smelled good, like wet moss in the woods. The air was fresher somehow when it rained. Then it grew into a full-blown thunderstorm. I've always loved a good thunderstorm. Mouse and Peanut, my two best friends, and the girls that were hanging out on Water Street hill ran for cover and I stood in the middle of the street with my arms spread out, looking toward the sky with my mouth wide open. I was never scared I'd be struck by lightning. I liked the feel of the hard rain stinging my skin through my shirt and I walked slow and deliberate steps toward home, loving the way the blacktop glistened and the leaves on the trees and bushes along the road had a slick and shiny look. And the next day and the next and the next, the rain continued. My parents complained after there had been enough to water the garden and soak into the ground to make the grass healthy and it kept coming.

"Water's gonna get high if it keeps on," my father said. And the rain was the topic of every conversation my parents had with other adults. I didn't mind it so much. I was a teenager, true enough, but still had enough kid in me to stomp in the puddles of water that pooled in the sinkholes in the road and to try to convince Peanut and Mouse to play basketball in the rain. The girls didn't come out much, though; I guess they didn't want to get their hair messed up. It rained so much that the bottoms began to flood and families who lived below had to evacuate their homes. Even the creamery that rested at the bottom of the hill had to evacuate. Me and my boys watched carloads of families grabbing what they could and moving toward higher ground. Saw the big milk trucks heading out with their last loads before the creamery shut down. We knew everything that happened on Water Street.

We also watched Daddy and Uncle Willie help old man MacIntosh and his boy move their raggedy living room suite, their beds and kitchen table into our garage for safekeeping. The MacIntosh women—a tall skinny mother, and an average-looking girl—both blonde-headed, wet from head to toe, carried garbage bags of clothes and other belongings up out of the water. They disappeared behind our house, returned empty-handed, and headed back down the hill for more.

My father looked like he had put in a day's work up at Uncle Willie's farm, his legs muddy to the knees. I caught Daddy's eye once but he lost sight of me when he stopped to wipe the sweat from his forehead and I was gone before he cleared his vision. I knew that I was only seconds away from getting called in to help with the white folks' disaster.

The rain stopped but everything was watery and shiny. There was a coolness in the air. Peanut had to go in to supper, but Mouse and I played street ball even after the sun went down, splashing the ball on the wet pavement. The rain stopping brought the girls back and it seemed like we played our hardest when the girls were watching. In between breathers, Mouse would walk up on the girls moving his hips and they would squeal and back away from him. I never did do that but I thought about it. When the girls screamed too loud or the music was up too high, Miss Sandy lifted the screen in her window and said, "Y'all little heathens need to take y'alls bad asses to bed! I'ma call every single one of your mothers and fathers!" But we always knew what she really meant was that we had at least one more chance to act civilized. If she raised that window a second time we all ran in our different directions home.

That night, before I went inside the house, I grabbed the

spare key to the garage from under the flowerpot and opened the door. The garage smelled of dampness like something about to mold. Inside there was our tiller, lawnmower, spare tires, tools, garden hoses, quilting horses... Everything had been pushed into the corners and squeezed up against the walls to make room. The only light I had to see by was the streaks of brightness that filtered into the side window from the utility light that stood in our backyard. I didn't switch on the garage light for fear that it would wake my parents.

In the darkness, I sat on the MacIntoshes' couch trying to picture the furniture in its proper place and them in their own living room. I leaned my head back into the cushion and closed my eyes but I couldn't quite bring the image into focus. Every time I tried, the MacIntoshes' bodies would transfigure into my own family, or Peanut's, or Mouse's, or the Patton sisters', somebody's I could see clearly. I moved to their kitchen table, which was set up like it was there to be used, and sat down in one of the wobbly wooden chairs. I tried to imagine myself at the MacIntoshes' dinner table; the old man's chin shaking mad.

Family photographs were spread out across the table like roof shingles, each with curling edges from the dampness. I held each of them up to the light to see the faces. I was surprised that the MacIntosh family photographs were similar to ours. Yellowed pictures of men dirtied with work, fresh from the tobacco fields. Their mouths calling for water, not smiles for the camera. Children captured on old-fashioned porches, along dirt roads, up against trees or prized vegetable plants. So many children in one weathered image, that the photographer obviously had a difficult time fitting all of them into the frame. I looked at the dark-haired boy whose half-face appeared at the edge and wondered how he felt years later, with only a portion of him being documented. The women wore the finest dresses they owned, refusing to be captured on film any other way. Probably wearing their favorites from some past Easter Sunday. Hats tilted to one side. Bows in their hair. Their faces lipsticked and rouged up. I sifted through the MacIntosh children's school photographs. Frozen poses that could have been Peanut's or mine. Any of us. I left those pictures in the garage but carried their impressions to bed with me that night.

I never knew where they had disappeared to, but on the first of May, the MacIntoshes returned. Repairs had been made to their house, and I watched from my upstairs bedroom window while they loaded their belongings into a moving truck and went back down the hill to get on with their lives. They brought people with them, relatives I supposed, to help with all the lifting and carrying. My mother was at the corner of the garage talking to Mrs. MacIntosh, both of them with hands on their hips. The boy and his sister stood back with their arms crossed and watched the adults crossing the color line again.

Sometimes I look at my students up at Lincoln and try to see inside their faces. I wonder what they really think. They are so jumbled up now. The white ones sitting with the black ones, the brown ones, the red ones, like that song from church—*Red and yellow, black and white, they are precious in his sight, Jesus loves the little children of the world.* But then, again, foul shit still happens too. I see the black and the brown kids get slighted by white teachers all the time. It's hard for me sometimes to keep speaking to my colleagues when I know what goes on in their classrooms. I come home burdened down with it all sometimes. I feel guilty if I sneak one of my black kids a piece of chocolate or a stick of gum or give them the benefit of the doubt on a test. I feel that something isn't right. Usually the next day I go back and I'm hard, tough as nails. I feel like I've got to show my own what it's going to be like on them. Feel like they need some reality so they're prepared, but that doesn't make me feel better either.

That summer, me, Mouse, Peanut and the Patton sisters landed jobs in the Upstart Program. Upstart was a summer work program for "underprivileged kids." Mama had a factory-wide layoff, but with Daddy's salary I barely qualified. Mouse and Peanut made it in easy. And I wasn't surprised at all to see the MacIntosh kids when we arrived.

During orientation, all the black kids sat together as usual.

Me, Mouse and Peanut on one side of the table, the Patton sisters on the other. The white kids were scattered throughout the room, divided up in their own self-made categories. Ones we couldn't figure out just by looking. We listened as intently as teenagers could to Mr. Pritchard drone on about the importance of a good work ethic.

"Say it with me," he said, his voice sounding like he had peanut butter on his tongue. "What kind of work does the Upstart Program expect from you?"

"Quality," we all said together with the enthusiasm of Sunday school.

"When are you to report for work?"

"On time."

"What are we going to do?"

"Complete our tasks to the best of our abilities."

Mr. Pritchard smiled each time we answered him in unison. His belly rose way out in front of him as he floated down the aisles between the tables, making sure we were paying attention. He reminded me of the whale I'd seen on Mutual of Omaha's *Wild Kingdom*, the night before. Only he was a whale in a pale green knit suit with brown rickrack running around the collar and a coffee-stained white shirt.

"And how ugly is my whale suit?" I was imagining him to say.

"Very ugly," we all said together.

Playing this game kept me awake and fully attentive.

"How bald am I?"

"Bald as a baby's white ass."

Me and my boys had anticipated a summer of watching the Patton sisters' asses twist in tight pants suits and mini dresses, so when we had our fifteen-minute breaks we admired them from afar, eating our fill of candy bars and potato chips from the snack machine. The Patton sisters weren't small girls by any means. They were big-boned, thick in the hips, the kind of girls we lusted over.

"Now Toni, that girl is fine," Mouse starts out. "She's the shit. Brothers! Can I get an Amen?!"

"Amen! Lord have mercy! Amen!" Peanut nudged me as Toni bent over to retrieve her ink pen as she entered the restroom.

Candy stood in the corner by herself munching a package of nabs, leaning quietly against the machine.

"I'm a breast man, myself, fellas," I said to my boys and nodded toward Candy. "Lookie, lookie, lookie here."

We giggled like kindergarteners.

"What is wrong with y'all fools?" Toni said coming from the bathroom, seeing us in a heap.

"Nothing," we said in unison.

"Nothing," Peanut said again. "Just that Junior and Mouse say you have one fine beeeehind."

"Y'all just nasty!" Toni said turning on her heels and joining her sister at the snack machine.

I elbowed Peanut in the ribs and we all laughed so hard we strained to keep from pissing on ourselves. The Patton sisters thought we were vulgar but we thought we were cool as hell.

At the end of the day, the five of us walked home together. We could see the MacIntosh kids behind us. Me, Mouse, Peanut and the Patton sisters were all assigned to the library so we celebrated all the way down the street, giving each other fives every way we knew how.

"Men at work" Mouse said rearing his shoulders back, tugging on his shirt collar, and doing a bad impression of a businessman.

"We gonna put some soul train up in the library, babeeee," Peanut said dancing around us in circles. "Doing the hustle and the bump up and down the history section." He rode his hip into Candy's and she pushed him away.

"Go on fool."

We took turns walking playfully with our arms around the Patton sisters until they shrugged our arms off their shoulders.

Toni hollered, "Boy, I ain't playing. You better get off me."

It was all cool, though, as long as we were in a group. None of us had gotten to the one-on-one stage.

Night found us telling our stories up on the hill. We caught up with the other kids' days. Summer chores, watching TV, eating their families out of house and home. I knew Yolanda back then, seems like I've known her my whole life. Her friend Mona, Jeanette Stokes, even my cousin Angie, Uncle Willie's granddaughter, who spent summers with us sometime—man there were a lot of us. We listened to music and danced in the street until Peanut rose up and said, "I don't know about y'all Negroes but this brother gots a j-o-b," and we would laugh, then scatter. Me and Mouse knew it was just time for Peanut to go home and eat his supper, but he played it off good and was all the cooler in our eyes for handling his business proper.

The first day of work was messed up. The MacIntosh kids were standing at the library counter when we arrived. The white women, who worked there, acted like they were afraid of us, especially the brothers. They avoided us as long as possible, whispering through their teeth the white woman's code: Smile at the niggers and they won't kill you.

Candy and Toni got their assignments first. They could type like lightning. The MacIntoshes got assigned to shelving books. And the brothers, we, got the shit work of unloading and unpacking boxes of books in a storage room that seemed to reach miles into the ceiling. We were pissed and almost quit but the thoughts of five hundred dollars at the end of the summer saved us from bailing. I knew that Timmy MacIntosh wouldn't have known what a duodecimal system was if it bit him in the ass and on the way home I let him know that. I had to, especially after a *double-dog dare* from my boys.

"Hey, white boy!" I hollered to him as we turned off Main Street.

"What, black boy?" he said his arms flying up like *What you gonna do about it?*

"What the fuck did you say?" I walked up on him chest-to-chest.

Timmy looked me straight in the face.

"I said, 'What?!'"

The white boy was holding his own.

Mouse nodded at me like: Handle your business, chump!

"Look jive ass punk," I said, poking him in the center of his chest. "Why you think you got your job? Tell us, white boy. Why?"

Peanut and Mouse had my back. They stood with their arms crossed ready to step in it if necessary even though I could see Peanut's hands trembling.

I stepped out of the white boy's personal space to give him some room to fuck up again. I was prepared, scared as hell, but prepared to take it all the way. But he walked away, dragging his sister down to their part of the street with him. He never looked back even with me screaming, "That's right hoogie, go on down to the water hole you, punk ass, muskrat."

The muskrat jab struck the Patton girls and the brothers as corny as hell but we still laughed.

It would be years later before I learnt that Timmy MacIntosh was one of the baddest white boys in Stanford. He could have probably cleaned the street top to bottom with my non-fighting black ass, Mouse and Peanut, too, if he had really wanted to. In high school, he got permanently expelled for fighting. Word was, he hurt somebody real bad. But I never knew any of that, that summer. Maybe he just wasn't feeling froggy that night.

By July, we had nearly brought in every box of books in the warehouse, the Patton sisters had typed the cards and Timmy and his sister, Julie, had placed them on the shelves. By then, I had developed a secret crush on Julie and I think she liked me too. We sat at a safe distance from each and talked small talk, when nobody was looking—mostly about school.

"Got Mrs. Duncan for English, next year?"

"No, Mrs. Reilly."

That's the kind of stuff we talked about. Nothing. I never told the fellas about Julie and me.

Once, in the warehouse, Julie and I were looking over the inventory sheet together and standing side by side and her hair brushed across my arm. Julie wasn't that pretty a girl but there was something about her, kind of a clumsy attraction, that didn't put her completely out of my league. She looked at me and I looked at her.

"What is it?" she said, laughing a flirty laugh.

"Nothing."

"It's something. Do I have a bump or something?"

"No, just a big booger hanging off your nose."

She punched me in the chest and I grabbed her shoulders.

"Girl..." I started laughing and was suddenly embarrassed that we were so close. I remember my first kiss growing from some goofy encounter like that, but Julie and I quickly separated. We exchanged furtive glances and silly laughs but kept a safe distance.

I think of Julie MacIntosh when I see little Sara and I wonder what would have happened between us if we had come up in today's world. Sara holds hands with black boys in school and nobody says a word. I wonder what her parents think. If they know. I watch Sara sometimes smiling, then looking away when she's talking to one of the boys and they are pressed together like a couple up against one of the lockers. I'm supposed to break up that sort of thing and I do, but sometimes I watch them for a while before I go over and ask them to move along to their next class. It's then that I think about Julie. If she ever gave me a second thought.

I saw the MacIntoshes coming and going all that summer. We did our thing. They did theirs. We shared a swimming hole one day down by the creamery but the white kids swam at one end. The black kids at the other. I watched Julie from afar but knew there was no way to get to her. By the time school started back, the MacIntoshes were the last thing on my mind. Yolanda and I were seniors and a couple.

I hadn't thought about Julie MacIntosh and that summer, until years later when I met a white woman at a party. I was still taking classes and hadn't graduated college yet. Me and Yolanda had been fighting off and on. Mouse had invited me to a party at one of his co-worker's houses. I'd drunk a few beers and Mouse had some woman held up in the kitchen, rapping his rap. I was standing near the door watching Mouse go through his thing, chuckling to myself and wondering how I was going to get home. Mouse seemed to be comfortable, but I felt out of place with us being the only two brothers there. A woman came over to me, flipped her hair over her shoulder and introduced herself. Julie came back to me in that moment, a blur of a young brother's past. A jolt of memory like cold water in the face. The woman was plain but pretty. Long brown hair and not a drop of makeup on her face. Young and dewy like I remember Julie being. Most of the other girls had on heels and were dressed up but this woman wore blue jeans, a T-shirt and tennis shoes.

"I'm Bonnie," she said extending her hand out for me to shake.

"Junior," I took her hand and shook the tips of her fingers because my hand was still wet from the beer can.

"Junior, you want to dance?"

My first inclination was to say, No. But just when she asked, the first R&B song I had heard since I walked in the place began to play. I looked at Mouse, who was now kissing the woman in the kitchen and pressing her up against the counter and decided, Why not?

In the center of the living room, the furniture was pushed up against the walls leaving the center open for dancing. Bonnie commences to winding her hips through the air before we even take our place. She smiles at me but we don't say anything, we just dance. There are other people dancing around us. I am waiting for someone to say something about a black man dancing with a white woman but nobody says a word.

"Yee-hah," someone yells from the corner and just about everyone follows suit. The song changes to rock and roll and the dancing transmutes into something that I didn't want to be a part of. I stop dancing cold in mid-stride. Bonnie laughs, grabs me by the hand and leads me through the crowd to the den.

"So, Junior," she says, "tell me about Junior."

"Ain't much to tell about Junior. Tell me about Bonnie."

"I work with Mouse."

"This your crib?"

"No that's another friend."

Bonnie goes on and tells me about her ex-husband and how

he came to be her ex. I am still not comfortable, but fairly interested, so I listen. Through the den I see Mouse slow dancing with the woman he's with. I watch him grinding against the blonde woman, with hair nearing her waist, and her grinding against him, dipping low during parts of the song, which lets me know they've done this before. Practiced.

When Bonnie sees me looking, she giggles and shakes her head. "Mouse and Karen, they're both a mess. We all work together. Tomorrow they won't know what hit them."

"Will you know what hit you?" I don't know what made me say that but I did.

"Depends on what hits me. Don't you think?" She moved into the space between us and kissed me long and hard.

"Damn," I pulled back from her a bit but wasn't fighting it too hard. "I don't know how in the hell I'm getting home? Don't look like my partner is going nowhere."

I got in Bonnie's car knowing full damn well that I couldn't get her to take me home. Yolanda was home waiting on me. So me and Bonnie ended up at a motel. The first time we tried to get going, I went limp as a dishrag. I was embarrassed but kind of relieved, but Bonnie wasn't giving up. I should have been thinking about Yolanda but I wasn't. Right then I was thinking of Lois Carter, the women at the library when I was a kid, about old man MacIntosh and everything my daddy had said about white people.

Years later, I tried to explain it to Yolanda.

"I want a divorce," she said calm and collected, which I think hurt me the most. If she had hit me or something, I would have felt better.

"Baby, I'm sorry," I tried to explain, reaching out to put my arms around her. "It was just something that happened one time, years ago. I was still in college then. I love you. I've never seen her again. Not since that night. I probably wouldn't even know her if she knocked on this door right now."

I was trying to be honest to save our marriage. I wanted to tell her everything. I wanted to tell her that it had nothing to do with her but that it stemmed from this thing in my head that has always made me wonder. I wanted her to be my best friend. But I knew she didn't want to hear that. I wouldn't have wanted to hear it either if I had been in her shoes.

"I love you. You know that."

Yolanda put her hands to her face and breathed into her hands. She didn't cry though.

"I love you too, but I want my divorce."

"No, you don't," I told her.

"What other secrets you got?"

"None," I said. "No other secrets."

I held her in my arms but she stood stiff and unyielding. She told me it wasn't going to work, but in the end I knew it would be all right. That night she let me hold her while we slept.

My wife is beautiful, whether she knows that or not. Don't get me wrong. I'm not bullshitting. Of course I've seen younger and I've seen prettier—but she's beautiful. She's brown-skinned and plain like one of God's creatures. I've known her forever and she's one of my best friends. I don't know what I'd do without her. When I look in her eyes, I can't explain it but I know we are a perfect fit.

That next morning we made love. After we were finished she asked me again.

"What other secrets you got?"

I answered that I had none and she named every woman we had ever known and asked me if I found them attractive. If I had ever slept with any of them. That's routine now. We go through this often.

"I married you," I say. "You, you, you," and I smile at her and sometimes flick her bare nipples—a *you* for each flick. And usually I can get her to smile but some mornings she stares off into the darkness. I feel her doubt in the space between us in the bed.

Yesterday, at school, I met Sara's parents at a parent-teacher's meeting. The father, a tall, military man, avoided eye contact and the mother, a homemaker in a red appliquéd sweater, made sure she placed her self away from me on the other side of the father. I knew the type, and when the father avoided my handshake, I knew for sure.

"Sara is doing well," I started my spiel, "but she could do much better."

The father glared at his daughter.

"She has a D right now and she's quite capable of A or B work."

"Do you think it's the company she keeps?" the mother asked.

I looked at Sara and she had moved herself away from her parents. She made sure there was space between the chairs.

"No, mom."

"Girl, you better get it in gear."

"Well, if she would just get her homework in. She has several zeros on her homework."

I leaned in and opened my grade book so they could see. The father leaned back in his chair and the mother peered at the grades and shook her head. They both stared down the row at their daughter.

"Sara, I know you can do the work." I didn't know what else to say.

"And you better get to doing it." The father leaned toward Sara and she slumped back down in her chair.

I thanked the family for coming in and assured them that Sara's grade could rebound if she just worked harder. As they left, I heard the father mutter, "Damned niggers."

"Excuse me, what did you say?"

"Come on, honey!" the wife urged.

The father stopped, then continued out the door. I felt like killing the son-of-a-bitch. Sara cried and looked at me with an apology she couldn't say.

Last night at home, I didn't eat dinner. I stared at my food and tried to calm myself down. I went out in the backyard and shot a few baskets.

Yolanda looked at me sideways and asked me what was wrong.

"Nothing," I said. "Just a tough day at work."

In bed, snuggled up with Yolanda, my mind raced to the past. I thought about the night I slept with Bonnie after that party. Sleeping with that white woman was surprisingly just like sleeping with a sister, same parts, same process. No lights, bells or whistles. Only difference was I felt so wrong for doing it. Not just because Yolanda was home waiting on me. The guilt of messing around on my wife would come later. Seemed like a part of me was prepared for the door to be broken down by a lynch mob. Another part of me felt like I had turned my back on my mother, Yolanda and every black woman I had ever known.

I ran out on Bonnie that night and never saw her again. But before I left, I stroked her hair in the dark and thought of Julie MacIntosh. It was 1979… In the end, when it was all over, Daddy and MacIntosh had shaken hands, my father even going so far as to pat the old man on the arm like I'd seen him do deacons in church. Julie looked up and noticed me in the window. I remembered Julie, skinny and stringy-haired, that spring day in the rain. I thought of the photographs of her people, who floated in my dreams that night. I could see her face clear as day. I looked back for just a minute before anyone noticed, then closed the curtain. She had shaded her eyes to get a better look at me, but before she caught my glance, I was already on my bed, wondering what her father had taught her about black folks.

When I hadn't fallen asleep in her arms and she could tell, Yolanda whispered, "Earth to Junior. Is anybody home?" and knocked on my head with her knuckles. She's a funny woman.

There was so much that I couldn't explain. Things I'd never be able to explain to my wife. Things I couldn't even explain to myself. I didn't know why all these memories popped into my mind. I knew she wouldn't understand if I tried to explain. So it was a secret I kept to myself and let the churning continue. Maybe one day I'd figure it all out.

I nodded my head *yes* and managed a brief, "Uh huh."

Yolanda pulled away from me and looked me in the face, her eyebrows rising up in a question, "You sure you okay?"

I love Yolanda. When I see the concern on her face, I squeeze her tight and realize how lucky I am to have her, to wake up to her smile every day and to sit down and eat breakfast with her and my beautiful daughter. In this house, I'm safe and secure.

"Don't make me worry about you?" she says.

"I'm fine," I said. "I'm here."

In Plain Sight

Jeanette

In Plain Sight

My mother talks to herself and to my father, who has been dead for twenty-four years. She's one of those women up in age, whose spine is starting to crook right between the shoulders. She speaks in tongues sometimes but she doesn't mean any harm, wouldn't hurt a fly. Mama is developing a shuffle when she walks. Wears mismatched outfits: pinstripes and prints, plaids and paisley. She's invisible. People just can't see my mother. Not since she shed her old skin in the mental hospital, the year my father died, and came back home wearing her pain on the outside, a woman to be avoided.

I nod and speak to the neighbors, but usually they just stare and watch me walk from the front stoop all the way to the door like I'm a parade with baton twirlers and mascots and a live marching band. The crazy woman's crazy daughter. Inside the house, I pull out the framed photograph we keep nested in pink tissue paper like a gift. It's hidden in the front of the closet just above the coat rack almost in plain sight.

We are captured in black and tan. I'm round on my mother's

lap in a sun suit. My father's arm is draped around Mama's bony little shoulders like a safety net. When I look at this photograph, I know Mama was a woman to be seen back then. There is something in her face that I barely remember, her head leans into my father's shoulder. I always take the photograph down, stroke the faces underneath the glass. Try to imagine my mother in full motion in her 'before' state. But mostly all I remember is the 'after.'

I crane my neck back to see my mother's face the night she left me. Her eyes are red as sunset. When I ask her what's wrong, she begins wailing. Reverend Townsend stops his Eldorado in front of a small, red brick apartment in Danville. As we exit the car, it's beginning to snow and a gust of wind penetrates through my coat, through the layers that my mother has plastered on my body: an undershirt, T-shirt, sweatshirt, and the fake fur that is always reserved for Sunday.

Mama takes my mitten-covered hand and leads me to the front door. Bertha Watkins, my mother's friend, lives in this apartment. She is younger than my mother. Her hair is pulled back tight in one big Afro puff. She is a bright-skinned woman with tiny wire-rimmed glasses that perch on her nose, the kind of woman who wears high heels around the house. She hugs my mother tight and whispers, "Take care of yourself, Barbara."

I am at their hips trying to grab onto something swirling through me that I can't explain.

Miss Watkins likes loud music. It blares from floor speakers. Al Green's voice croons so loud that it's just one turn of the knob below painful to the ears, nothing like Mama's gospel or Daddy's Nat King Cole collection. Miss Watkins moves to the beat of that music like she's dancing from couch to kitchen. All her doorways are covered with long rows of colorful wooden beads that swish together like waterfalls when I walk through them. I'm dancing too.

She lets me eat things my mother doesn't. S'mores and popcorn, hot dogs and fruit cocktail for dinner. Butter pecan ice cream for breakfast. She gives me a bubble bath poured from a pink bottle that smells like roses. She sits on the edge of the tub, lathers me up like I'm a baby, her soapy hand sliding along my collarbone, and feeds me red grapes while I soak in the bubbles. When I look at her she reminds me of Diahann Carroll playing Julia on TV, only Miss Watkins is a Diahann Carroll with more soul.

Miss Watkins asks me what's wrong and I shrug my shoulders.

"Come on, Shug, come here to Bertha," she says and spreads her arms open like a rainbow.

"Where's my mama at?" I ask, trying to be determined not to give in to my melting insides.

"Your mama'll be back before you know it," she tells me and rubs up and down my arms as affectionately as a hug. She grabs my hands together into hers and rests them on my lap. But I just nod instead of smiling; won't speak a blessed word out loud.

Later that night, in Bertha's spare room, I hear voices in the heating grate. On my hands and knees I try to see through the grate thinking that there are tiny people down there. By the time Bertha comes back in to check on me, my imagination has turned wild and I am shaking from fear of whoever lives under her floor. Bertha takes me down the hall and puts me in her bed. She is dressed in a white silky nightgown and high-heeled house slippers.

In her sitting room there is a man on the sofa dressed in a sky blue suit. He is a pretty man. Long wavy charcoal hair pulled back in a ponytail. A face as pretty as any woman I have ever seen.

"Baby, this is Barbara Jean's child, Jeanette," Bertha says. "The one I told you about," she says and they look at each other.

"Hello," the pretty man says and nods.

"Good night, Miss Jeanette," he says, cupping his hand next to his mouth like he's telling a secret and laughs at his own silliness.

As Bertha hurries me along, a sweet smoky smell wafts through the apartment and a slow song, one I don't remember the name of, one by the O'Jays, is playing on the record player.

Warm in Bertha's bed, I begin to await my mother's return. The quiet is broken by haughty laughter and the sound of the plastic record player arm lifting from the record. A part of me floats in the music. The record player turns itself off and I ease out of bed. I see Bertha's face and bare shoulders, a bit of breast, rising up and down from the back of the sofa. I hear the pretty man's voice but I can't see him. He is making sounds as round as an egg beneath Bertha's writhing dance. Her eyes are barely shut, her head tilted back like Diana Ross waiting for Billy D's kiss in *Mahogany*. I think Bertha is the most beautiful woman I have ever seen. More beautiful than Diahann Carroll and Diana Ross and all the women in JET magazine. I watch until Bertha's head and torso disappear into the sofa, where the pretty man waits for her; then I crawl back into bed.

Later, I hear the front door close. The wooden beads rain down on Bertha as she moves from room to room. The sounds of a bath, her feet moving across the carpet, then, suddenly I smell her, like fresh rose petals, beside me in the bed. I am feigning sleep and feel her breath against my cheek. Her hands through my hair.

"Bless her heart," she whispers before she turns her back from me to sleep. In the dark, I stare into the back of her head until I drift off.

The last time my father comes to me in flesh and blood, he is wearing his gray work uniform and he's just home from the printing factory. Daddy is a big man, his hair getting snowy at the edges. A handsome man dipped in honey, more pretty than Bertha's man. I picture that last night, see my father's image moving away from me toward the door. He briefly looks back. His hand, big and brown, looking like love to me, is the last part of him I see as he brings the door to a close. When I am told the other details of that night—my father falling from the couch; the pain in his chest; my mother's screams; the ambulance; the doctor's northern accent thick and full of compassion, telling my mother there was nothing they could do—it always seems to me that the bearer of the memory is making the story up. Or that it's a television movie and none of it happened at all. Not in anybody's real life any way. I don't remember the hospital, the doctor, nurses and kinfolk holding my mother up when she fainted with grief. I don't remember knowing my father was dead.

"She commenced seeing things before that man was cold in the morgue," relatives say of my mother. "She loved your daddy like no other love I've ever seen."

That is the kind of love I see in my mother's eyes when she stares out at me from that hidden photograph. I don't remember any of the horror of the night my father died, even though they all say I was there. Seems like I went to sleep when Daddy died and woke up at Bertha Watkins' door, smitten with her ability to show me what living was all about.

Mama told Bertha not to take me to the service, that I was too young to see death. My mother didn't attend Daddy's funeral either. She was in the hospital. Of course I never witnessed her stay but still I see glimpses of my mother in a straightjacket like *One Flew Over the Cuckoo's Nest,* a team of psychiatrists trying to convince her that her dead husband really was dead. It caused a fit in the family that me and Mama were out of pocket for Daddy's funeral, but I am sure that Daddy's spirit visited both of us that day. Somehow I know it was okay with him if we weren't there to see his empty body.

My father had been buried for a month when my mother came back to claim me. She returned as somebody even I didn't recognize—a spirit barely alive imprisoned in her body, a husk. When we returned home, I mourned as much for the loss of my mother as I did for my father. Even then her shoulders had started to slump in surrender. Her skin had begun to wrinkle.

"Barbara Jean, honey, I'm so sorry," Bertha Watkins told my mother. "Call if you need anything else," she said, one bangled hand on her hip, the other holding my belongings in a brown paper sack.

Mama looked Bertha right between the eyes and said, "Berth, John Junior is just fine."

Bertha looked at my mother like she was a stranger. And she was.

"John Junior, get Jeanette and let's head to the house," my mother said to my father's ghost.

"Just call me if you need anything," Bertha said again, her

eyebrows wrinkled in confusion. "I'll keep Jeanette anytime. She's a sweet child."

But Mama never called on Miss Watkins again and Bertha Watkins never called Mama. My mother in her 'after' condition was too painful for anyone to look at, at too close a range. No amount of medicine or psychotherapy could cure my mother from fixing a plate of food for my dead father every night and having conversations with him. Sometimes at night I heard her laughing: "John Junior quit acting a fool." But it was long before then that I realized that my mother was no longer there. That she had died with my father. I was a little girl being raised by spirits.

In the beginning, when people would come over to see if we needed anything, Mama would answer the door, the wild look in her eyes already developed, and say, "No thank you, John Junior'll be home before too long, I'll get him to mow the yard." Or rake the leaves, or fix the front gate, or trim the trees. I was grateful when Reverend Townsend sneaked over every couple of months to fix something broken, to clean the gutters or replace the siding. Mama would come to the door and catch him in the act.

"Reverend Townsend leave that alone now. John Junior will be off work in an hour and he's gonna do that."

"It's all right," he would holler back in his most convincing preacher voice. "He told me to go ahead and get started without him."

Mama would nod and close the door like she knew Reverend Townsend's words to be true fact. Sometimes I stood out on the porch and watched Reverend Townsend do the things my father used to do. I also knew he brought the food sacks and money that would appear in our screen door and in our mailbox. I never knew why he did these things but back then I often thought it was his religious duty to be mindful of spirits.

By the time I was in junior high, I was looking for a doorway to pass through back to the living. Looking for magic, a love as powerful as the love my parents shared. The kind of love I could die for, but also something more. Something that would just give me a piece of the stirrings that Bertha Watkins possessed.

Until those middle school years, everything I knew about my peers or that they knew about me was bits of overheard conversation. My ears were always perked and alert although I kept my eyes down most of the time. I knew before the other girls when Mona had sex with Yolanda's brother. I knew about the touchy-feely games they all played on Water Street hill. About Mrs. Farley, our home economics teacher, and her female problems, and I certainly knew what they all thought about me. Weird. Too quiet. That my mother was "kinda off."

In seventh grade, Eric Brown came up to me and asked, "You the one that lives in the haunted house?"

"Haunt this," I said and raised my skirt, pulled down my panties and showed him my pubic hair. This incited hoops and hollers from the other students and suspension from school for a week. After that, my mother was rarely mentioned.

At night, I would sneak out of the house and hang out with the other teenagers on Water Street. Eric, his friends called him Peanut, was the first boy I kissed. The other girls kissed with their mouths shut, but when I kissed I was searching for an abyss in which I could escape through. By the time I got to Mouse, I was letting boys touch my breasts and rub between my legs. It was during those times that I could see the opening to a doorway out. I was a breathing person, not the ghosts my parents were. I imagined myself like Bertha Watkins. Real. My eyes almost closed, a writhing dance on some boy's fingertips, his mouth open like an O, leaving my flesh torrid and wanting. I developed a reputation and the boys kept coming, but it never went past this touching game, which I had designed just to know that I was among the living.

After high school, I moved to Danville for work. I tried to look Bertha up but she had moved. I even peered in her old apartment window and asked the neighbors.

"She been gone."

"Do you know where?"

"Nope."

Then doors would shut. Sometimes someone would recognize me. "You Barbara Jean's daughter from over in Stanford, Water Street, right?"

Sometimes I said yes. Sometimes no. Same look either way. Eyeballs away, eyebrows up.

I settled into a job as a copy assistant at the paper. There I was free to create myself a world. I knew everything I needed to know about so many lives. I bought myself a new wardrobe and fashioned myself, keeping an eighties version of Bertha Watkins in mind. I was finally freed from my parents, except when I crept home for holidays and the occasional weekend to check on my mother.

I was too busy to have boyfriends but I did have a few failed attempts: dinner with the sports desk manager, a movie with the guy who delivered the large reams of paper that rested on the dock floor of the press room, the bespectacled librarian who lived in the B side of the duplex I lived in. In each case it was the same. Eventually they wanted to know about my past. "Tell me about your parents," they all would lead into, thinking they were making first-date small talk. And then I would make up a story, finish the date, but know I would never see them again.

From that distance, I was closer to my mother than I'd ever been. We would talk on the phone and she would describe for me the crocuses blooming along the side of the house, or how the sunlight made shadows along the wood floors or the song of the whippoorwill in the backyard. During those times, I would cradle the phone and imagine myself a life with a mother and father—all happy like those smiling television shows that captured my attention on Friday nights. Mama would often recite the circumstances of my birth, how many hours she was in labor, what she was wearing, how her belly button popped out like a flower blossom; or she'd tell me how much she and daddy were in love when they married. "I love your father with my whole me," she said.

Sometimes I might get a full conversation out of her that sounded normal, but it never failed that she would lapse into a long annotated conversation with my father, sometimes even a "lover's spat." Most of the time I would hang up the phone but sometimes I would sit and eavesdrop, listening to my mother's part of the back and forth. It was much easier to hear than it was to watch. Somehow it comforted the homesickness that would rise up in my gut from time to time, gnawing on my stomach, urging me home—a sudden seizure of calm that I couldn't understand or shake.

Two years after I started my job, I quit. Reverend Townsend called about my mother's condition. I came home to find Mama in a hospital hooked up to machines, the beat of her heart growing slower and slower. When I arrived, she rose up, removed the breathing mask from her face and said, "Go home girl, you're too young to see death." It was not the time for it but I laughed out loud seeing that Mama, somehow, failed to notice that I had lived with death all my life.

That night, as I held watch by my mother's bedside, my father came to me. He stood beside me watching Mama sleeping, not looking older than the day he died, younger in fact, like he had been on a vacation. He was not opaque like television ghosts but seemingly there in the flesh. I thought he was there for Mama but he turned to me.

"Daddy?"

"Ain't you a sight," Daddy said. "My girl all grown."

Is that really you, Daddy? I wanted to say but I couldn't release any of the mountains of words I had in reserve for a moment like this. Never thought I'd get a chance. I sat there watching my father for a long time but I didn't speak. I just watched him like you watch a bird that has landed close, afraid to move or speak less the creature take flight. He didn't say anything else, but stood staring down at Mama until a nurse came in to check her vitals. When the nurse flicked the light on, my mother roused up and said, "Where's John Junior? He was just here a minute ago."

The nurse looked at me and shook her head, a "poor dear" gesture. And I was still caught between the two worlds.

A woman doctor with round, dark eyes and skin like molasses came in the next morning. She checked all the gadgets and hoses, pulled out her stethoscope to double-check the readings of the monitors, and looked first at the chart, then down at the floor before she cleared her throat with concern.

"I'm sorry," she told me, her head bowing so low I could see the whiteness of the part in her jet-black hair. "Her heart is growing weaker."

I wanted to tell her that Mama had been dead for years but I knew she wouldn't understand. As she was explaining it all to me in medical terms, I was thinking about her, the doctor. I had overheard her telling another patient's family that she was originally from India. How did she feel about being here, way across the waters? I wondered. Was her mother waiting somewhere? Her father? All the doctors in the hospital were from all over the country, the world in fact, but here they were all foreigners. I knew I was one too.

I moved back home and got on with the weekly paper. I found a two-bedroom apartment just off Main Street that I decorated with furniture from my apartment in Danville, and some of Mama's furniture from the old house on Water Street—Mama's dinette set, couch, and the bed that had been hers and Daddy's for the spare room.

I was up at the Lexington Mall one weekend picking up my new lamp, when I saw Bertha Watkins. She was a little older but still had lights in her eyes and bangles on her wrists.

At first she didn't recognize me but then she screamed, "Little Jeanette Stokes!" the lilt of her voice carrying me in its palm. She handed her young, handsome boyfriend her bags. She told me she lived in Lexington and loved the city, while the boyfriend looked on with shy, hazel eyes. As she walked away she nodded her head toward the boyfriend, winked her eye and grinned a feisty smile. I wanted to hug Bertha Watkin's neck and tell her I still carried her with me like a favorite handkerchief tucked between my breasts but I didn't.

In the weeks that followed, I kept my eyes peeled for Mama's second coming. I had hoped she would come back a sprightly vision, her and Daddy two-stepping around the old couch. But I don't think we have choice in the spirits who haunt us. We have to settle for what we get. And I have.

An Ordinary Man

Reverend Townsend

An Ordinary Man

Before becoming a preacher, Reverend Townsend had been a deacon, and before becoming a deacon he had been simply Eli Henry Townsend, an ordinary man.

Eli, the boy, overgrown and clumsy for his age, with splotchy skin, and raggedy clothes still lives inside of Reverend Townsend, who is now over six feet tall and has broad shoulders, a belly that rises out in front of him under perfectly tailored suits. He doesn't look fat at all. He carries his weight well. Possesses a dignified strut.

The women in the church consider him good-looking when he peers at them over his wire-rimmed glasses and smiles at them above a well-groomed salt and pepper beard and says, "Yes, sister, how may I help you today?" His hellos sound like sermons. The entire community comes to him, the women mostly, to vent their problems and they dress to the nines. Reverend Townsend likes to see them in their suits and their colorful dresses—crisp and pleated, straight from the cleaners. Even when he tries not to, he takes great pleasure in a bit of cleavage or the fine ridges of a perfect neck bone that rises up daintily from a scooped collar or protrudes in a perfect angle from beneath an unbuttoned blouse. Women are a mystery to him. Fascinating.

He is mostly available on Sundays after church but he also schedules Thursday counseling sessions if they need him. He is precious to this cluster of women who dote on him and bring him sweet potato pies and lemon cakes, fried chicken and green beans, homemade rolls and cornbread.

And it isn't always one-sided. Reverend Townsend gives back to the community. He takes food to the sick, the elderly and the shut in. He cuts the yards of the widowers, drives folks to the doctor. He visits the nursing homes, conducts house visits and gives prayer. This is his life now.

Eli, the boy, remembers growing up in Hustonville, the death of his mother, he and his brother peering in the back room while she was on her deathbed. He was scared of her, afraid of the rattle that whistled in her throat. He strains his memory to see his mother smiling and happy like the mothers in his church but all he can glimpse is a woman rotting away in the bed as he watched from the doorway, her black hair splayed out on the pillow, her form hollow beneath the sheet. He sees his father, sitting at the kitchen table silent and angry, staring off into the dark, barking out orders to do chores when he opened his mouth.

Eli quit school in fourth grade to help his father on the farm. He remembers eating only fried potatoes and cornbread for supper. When he thinks of those days he goes to his refrigerator and checks to see if he still has a carton of eggs, a gallon of milk, meat, and he runs his fingertips over the canned vegetables and stews and soups in the cupboard, taps the boxes of crackers and snacks.

Eli, the boy, recalls some glimmer of play—he and his brother, Edward, playing baseball with rotten crab apples or pawpaws.

After the death of their mother, Eli and Edward should have grown closer and became each other's lean-to but it never happened like that. Whether it was a fight over a baseball game or a tug-of-war over who was to get the last piece of cornbread, there was always a wedge between them. A clear line drawn that neither of them crossed. Their father saw it, saw it plain as he saw the sun setting over the hills, but he never let on, never stopped the fight; never took sides. His grieving-well was dug too deeply.

If there was anything that Eli and Edward agreed on it was that grief murdered their father five years to the day after their mother had died. The doctors had said it was lung cancer from the cigars he smoked but anyone who knew him knew it was the grief.

After their father died, Edward, who was nineteen, took on his fifteen-year-old brother to raise. They kept up the farm as best they could, planted a garden and kept the chickens fed. They sold them in town on the weekends. Even then, in their orphaned state, Eli and Edward were opposites. Eli, even with all his hard work, cooked, cleaned, studied his mother's bible and carried it with him from place to place. He was still clumsy and unsure then, a heavy boy who was considered the nice one but not the handsome one. Edward worked odd jobs to make ends meet. Sometimes he worked over in Liberty at the sawmill, at others he traveled to Danville and Stanford for construction work, housing tobacco, cutting hay, just whatever he could get. He was a drinker and cursed to the high heavens but was the looker. A rugged, muscled torso and arm muscles that made girls speechless and flirty.

Reverend Townsend is fifty-six and single but has a girlfriend—Ariel.

Ariel is one of the church's finest. They do not make public appearances together because Reverend Townsend does not think it proper. She has gone to him every Wednesday evening after prayer meetings for six months. Some Wednesdays Reverend Townsend gets so beyond himself knowing what will come later with Ariel that he stutters in the prayer room when he notices her glancing in his direction. Ariel is a secretary at the elementary school. She is quiet and bookish. Not a drop of makeup, a member of the choir. She is forty-nine and never married and still lives with her parents.

She arrives at 6 P.M. carrying her church bookkeeping notebook. She enters the side door of Reverend Townsend's small two-bedroom parsonage.

"Good evening, Reverend," she says.

"Sister Ah-re-el. Please come in." A greeting fit for public.

Once inside, Reverend Townsend removes the notebook from Ariel's hands and places it on the kitchen table. He kisses not just the center of the back of her hand like the gentlemen do in the movies, but her palms and each of her fingers and up her arms to the elbows. He cradles her face in his hands and presses his lips to her eyelids, her cheeks and her nose. He places several closed-mouth kisses on her lips and lastly he moves to her neck. She has perfect neck bones, tiny, delicate ridges rising up below her sleek smooth skin. He unloosens the chignon neatly pinned on the back of her head and lets her hair fall to her shoulders. He strokes the nape of her neck, and lets her loose curls caress his hands but goes no further. He loves Ariel. She is cherished. Ariel receives this attention with a whispered, "Oh Reverend," and not much more.

Ariel is a quiet lover. In fact they are not lovers at all. Even though he is a perfectly fine cook, Ariel cooks dinner for Reverend Townsend. Spaghetti with fresh tomatoes and meat sauce with garlic biscuits one week, baked chicken and her special cheddar cheese potato casserole the next. It is a post she wishes to have permanently, not just on Wednesdays, but Reverend Townsend has not proposed.

Over dinner Ariel tells Reverend Townsend of her day. She tries to think of things to sound exciting but it always comes out the same.

"How was your day, Ah-re-el, dear?"

"The children at the school need the Lord."

"Well you should invite them to the Lord, Sister Ah-re-el."

"Where there is a will, there is a way. With God all is possible."

"Amen." Reverend Townsend nods his head because he is proud that Ariel is doing God's work.

After dinner has been served and eaten, the dishes washed and placed neatly away back underneath the pine cabinets, they settle on the couch with a good amount of respectable space between them.

Reverend Townsend tells Ariel about his dream of a church with a large congregation and a choir that travels all over the state and a separate young people's service with more music and basketball tournaments and respectable dances and socials for the children. She listens and can imagine her position beside him as the preacher's wife.

She tells him of her ambition to work with youth, her ideas about Sunday school, and sometimes she helps him through a rough spot in his sermon.

And so it goes. They are boring and formal in their love. Bland conversation laced with scripture. There is not one word about the personal that seeps out into their exchanges though they both want more.

Ariel wants to tell Reverend Townsend that he has the most kissable lips she has ever seen. She wants him to just tell her that he cares for her, that he loves her. She dreams of him on bended knee with a ring and the whole bit. Ariel seems content with their distant physical relationship but it is Reverend Townsend who desires to undo the buttons of her blouse and take her rosebud nipples into his mouth. He knows they are there. Sometimes he can see them, there, through her white blouses, waiting. When she is bent over the sink and he is in the den reading scripture out to her, he watches her thin hips straining the material of the long skirts she wears and he wants nothing more than to see and touch what's underneath. The rest is there. He loves her. He has tasted her cooking. He wishes she would tell him all her hopes and dreams. He wants to hear every word. He wants to have her in his arms. Much of the evening is a blur because Reverend Townsend is waiting for the night to end. He will miss Ariel when she leaves but he is anxious for the end when he will feel permission to touch Ariel goodbye.

Some nights when Ariel is wishing so much to be proposed to, she looks Reverend Townsend in the eye and leans her head into the back of the couch and tries to look alluring.

"I enjoy you," she says, a brave move for such a pious woman. It's *I love you* that she wants to say but she doesn't dare.

"You are a fine woman, Sister Ah-re-el. A good, good woman." And Reverend Townsend takes both of Ariel's hands into his and holds them firmly then kisses them again.

When she leaves at nine o' clock, Reverend Townsend helps her into her jacket and puts his arms around her waist. He is guilty of bringing his hands as close to her breasts as possible without actually touching them when he releases the hug. He will pray on that later. He kisses her again and wills himself not to act out of passion.

Once he hears her car start and move down the street, Reverend Townsend presses himself against the couch where the warmth of her body still lingers. He can smell the freshly showered cleanness of her skin.

One night Ariel leaves her sweater draped over the sofa chair and Reverend Townsend brings it into his bed and spreads it out near the pillow where Ariel should be. He tucks the covers up around where Ariel's neck would lie on the pillow and falls asleep with his hand cradling his head staring at the empty sweater-woman he has made.

He tries his best not to become desperate or vulgar but he really can't help it. He grasps for what he can't have. When Ariel leaves an open soda on his coffee table, he drinks the warm liquid, imagining he is taking in some of her essence. He allows his tongue to touch the opening of the can. He knows no one is in the room, yet he looks around to make sure. On the rare occasions when Ariel's blouse is extremely sheer or her skirt is tighter than he can stand or when he is lucky enough to accidentally touch her breasts, Reverend Townsend retreats to the bathroom to relieve himself by bringing his lust to completion. Afterward, the guilt rises up in him and he takes a shower, hoping to wash his indiscretions down the drain. He gets on his knees and prays before he climbs into his bed alone.

A teenaged Eli remembers Trena Mullins, his first girlfriend. There have not been many. Trena lived a few houses away on the quiet, winding street. Almost all the houses in Hustonville were spread out unevenly along the streets; there were no subdivisions, no bland, identical rows of houses. Across the street from the homes and rising up behind them in the back was farm property. Each family owned their own little front piece and back piece of land.

Trena wasn't the prettiest girl. She had buck teeth with short, uneven hair—a girl who was Eli's full twin in clumsiness and his opposite in girth, a tiny-waisted thing. He remembers their walk up through the woods behind his house. The smell of honeysuckle and wet grass. The sky bright blue as a robin's egg. The memory of the warmth of the sun on his face, the splash of the branch that trickled along the ground, and the sweetness of the blackberries they ate straight from the vine. He had shared his first kiss with Trena. Her lips had been like cotton.

Eli, the teenager, remembers his brother having girlfriends in the house all the time. Women, according to Edward, were there to cook and clean and to have sex with, because that was what they were good for. Occasionally a girlfriend would knock on the door when Eli was home alone. He would invite her in to watch the tiny black and white TV, offer her a bite to eat, something to drink, until Edward arrived home from the job. When Edward was around the girl would somehow transform, smoothing her hair over her ears, pressing her lips together to refresh her lipstick, giggling a new laugh. While she was alone with Eli, she was sweet and normal and prodded him for information about Edward. "Come on Eli, you can tell me," she would say and grab his arm playfully at the bicep.

Eli hadn't learned much about being a man from his father or from Edward. He hadn't learned much about women from them either. From his father he learned that women are fragile things that die like berries on the vine when you love them the most. From Edward he learned that women had a place in the world, a tiny place, like a pocket where you kept them held hostage until you needed them for something useful. He knew he wanted more than that from Ariel but he didn't know how to go about getting it. He wanted and needed so much from her that it filled up his whole parsonage. It was more than the cooking or the cleaning—more than the sex too—and he wanted it all.

For Eli's eighteenth birthday Edward brought home a loud-talking woman with wide hips. It was the first time Eli had ever seen a black woman with blonde hair.

"Happy birthday, little brother. This here is Candy Bridgewater. She's your present."

Eli, at first, was unsure exactly what Edward meant and when he realized, he couldn't do anything but look to the floor, embarrassed and even a bit frightened.

"Candy's gonna give you your first piece of pie. You ready for some birthday pie, boy?" Candy Bridgewater's voice boomed like thunder through the house. She kissed Eli long and hard and thrust her tongue in and out of his mouth. Eli tried to will himself to stop feeling what he was feeling but it was a lost cause. His embarrassment was growing and becoming obvious.

"I think he's ready, go have at it," Edward grinned and pointed down the short hallway to Eli's room and laughed.

In his room, Eli watched as Candy stripped off naked. He had never seen a woman's naked body before. Although Candy was twenty-five, a mother, and slightly out of shape, Eli took in her body like rain. "Touch me," she said when she got closer to the bed. She smelled like vanilla. He obeyed and touched her but when she tried to climb on top of him he stopped her, even though he didn't know why, but he felt so wicked. A few minutes later, he heard his brother forcing Candy up against the wall to finish the job she was paid to do. While he listened to the thump, thump, thump of Candy and Edward, Eli put his hand into his jeans and finished himself. That has been nearly forty years ago and still Reverend Townsend is a virgin and thankful to God for the will and the power to abstain. If he had been Catholic he would have been primed for the priesthood but as a Baptist he considered himself a rare specimen, a man worthy of God.

On the eve of their sixth-month anniversary, Ariel comes to Reverend Townsend like every Wednesday but when she enters the parsonage, she whisks past him, throws the notebook onto the counter, and begins dinner. She does not wait for the kissing ritual. She knows she will make him a perfect wife but he resists. She is tired of keeping her distance in church while the other women in the congregation fawn all over him. She is tired of the charade.

"Good evening, Sister Ah-re-el we missed you at prayer meeting," the Reverend manages but he is startled and taken aback.

"Reverend," she nods from across the room.

Reverend Townsend holds out his arms and walks toward her as if to try and reclaim his weekly hug but Ariel flits out of his grasp and begins preparing dinner. She takes out the cutting board and a large knife and pulls the head of lettuce from the refrigerator. The force she uses to prepare the greens causes the Reverend to take a few steps backward. His heart is beating miles and miles a minute. Something has come over Ariel.

"And how was your week?" Reverend Townsend stutters through the question, his voice quivering like Eli, the boy. He quickly clears his throat and tries to regain his self-respect.

"Fine." And Ariel brings the knife down so hard into the cucumbers that it makes a clunking sound. She pulls the chicken from the refrigerator, rinses it, and adds garlic, salt and pepper with the same rigid force, like a woman gone mad. Ariel is hoping that Reverend Townsend will come to her and take her into his arms but he doesn't. He retreats to the couch, where he pulls his reading glasses on and begins to read his sermon silently.

Ariel and Reverend Townsend exchange glances a few minutes apart all the while Ariel is preparing the food and making huffing and hissing sounds through her teeth. Reverend Townsend is trying to remain calm but the thought of losing Ariel sends his head into a spin. At the dinner table Ariel and Reverend Townsend eat in silence. He wants to ask her what is wrong but doesn't quite know how to on any personal level, so he begins the way that he would begin a counseling session with one of his church members.

"What burdens your heart, Sister Ariel? With God's help…"

"Reverend Townsend, I need to be going along." Before the dishes are washed and put away, before dinner is over, Ariel stands and begins to leave.

When Ariel reaches the door, her hand on the knob, Reverend Townsend, grabs her from behind at the shoulders. He still hasn't found the words yet. A man who depends on words for his salvation and he can't form a single word in his mouth. He pulls Ariel into him and holds her tightly around the waist. He is breathing heavy as though he is fighting for his life. Ariel leans back into him and gasps, "Eli," with surprise. He presses his mouth eagerly into her neck. He is sobbing and desperate, both decadent and pure. He allows his hand to move into her blouse and he carefully cups one of her breasts. He lets the weight of it rest in his hand like an egg.

Between Men

Mouse

Between Men

Kak Simpson's bootleg house wasn't a place where I was supposed to be, but at sixteen I was the youngest one in there. I settled myself among a handful of right good family men with wild sides, who got drunk on overpriced beer and laughed harder and told more lies than usual.

Kak, the first brotha I knew with sandy hair and freckles, owned the little one-bedroom house up off Maxwell Street. Kak hadn't worked a day in his life but paid his light bills and house note by selling booze to a handful of friends. Stanford was dry and Kak drove his truck up to Richmond every Thursday night and bought enough beer and whiskey to take everybody through the weekend. Kak's liquor was double, sometimes triple, what the men would have had to pay had they made the drive themselves, but there was more to it than that.

Kak's house was poorly lit by a lamp that sat on the floor of the living room. The furniture was spare. There weren't that many brothas in the house, but with somebody's ass on every free space on the couch and all the kitchen chairs filled, Kak always had to bring in a few lawn chairs from the back. He had a little set up back there.

If you hadn't known it not to be true, in the summertime, with Kak pretending to be a real bartender and the Christmas lights strung up around the patio, you would think you were in a nightclub. Especially when the blues hit the right notes and one of the old cats would get to dancing with an air partner, drunk as a skunk.

The first time I went into Kak's I was eight years old and went there with my daddy who had taken me to Kak's to toughen me up. "Boy you're a punk," he'd say. "Up under your mama all the damn time." Back then, I stood in the corners watching and listening, trying to keep my insides from coming back up into my mouth from the stench of sweat, stale smoke and open plastic cups of whiskey warming in the sun. I took in all them familiar dark faces with their tongues letting loose of stories of all the pussy they landed, and their knee slapping jokes.

That night when I was sixteen, I bought my own overpriced beer, draining each can in tall-man gulps. Daddy was gone but I let on like it didn't hurt me none. I was sixteen and my own man. When I was working my after-school gig, bagging groceries at Carter's, sometimes I'd see Old Man Boone, Ramey Lake, or one of the bootleg regulars in the line, and we'd share a nod, an understanding between men.

Old Man Boone would stand behind his wife, out of her sight, and grin and nod at me like I was his son who'd done good. He'd wink a knowing wink. When he came in by his self he'd whisper to me that he'd see me later—his breath still clean and sober before he made his way toward Kak's. Old Man Boone was a closet drinker, lived his life out in the open as a mailman and a deacon, then slipped over to Kak's to wipe his stress away. If you look real close though, around the eyes, you can always tell a drinking man a mile away, especially if you're one yourself. You can always spot your own kind even from a distance.

Ramey Lake was out in the open with his: a straight-up drinking man. He had the rep of a drunk, the kind of fella that the whole town turned their backs on. I'm not even sure that Old Man Boone prayed for Ramey on Sunday mornings. Looking back, I sure hope he did. Ramey's life was a hard one. He was almost always drunk but he worked when he could. Construction one day. Tobacco or hay the next. Depended on the season and how much juice he had in him. Folks around here say he used to have a wife and kids. They say the old woman ran off with the kids to her people up in Hazard but I never did hear Ramey talk about a wife or kids. Not one time. Ramey was one of them bachelors, the kind that warmed up canned food for supper every night. When I got older and he got up in age I'd go by his house and be just mouth-gaping speechless. Ramey sprawled out on a ratty old couch, the smell of piss and rotten food throughout the house. Bags of trash strewn all over, like he hadn't took the trash out to the curb for years. A bowl of uneaten chicken noodle soup molding on the table. Heard Miss Sandy was some kin to him but she never acted like it that I knew of. He's in the old folk's home now. Ramey's in poor shape.

Even back then, Old Man Boone and Ramey Lake seemed weak and feeble to me, gray hairs peeking from their heads, walking slow and steady. But now when I think about it they weren't old men at all. They were just drunk on their asses. They were men my Daddy's age then, fifty, not much more.

A hard life will age any man. I'll be there soon myself. Not too far away from it. In ten or fifteen years, some younguns gonna be looking at me the same way.

My life ain't been that hard. Been right here all this time. I ain't been nowhere. Ain't going nowhere. You ask the right person and they'd probably say that I'm an alcoholic. You ask me and I'd say I'm a brotha who has potential. Never too late. Even my mama says so.

My friends got out like fat rats. Junior's a big man in town, a schoolteacher and all. Peanut's a...well, hell, I don't know what Peanut is...don't know where he is. He's way off somewhere doing good I heard. One of them office types. First one then the other of our bunch has gotten married and divorced. Some of them two and three times over. All but me. I ain't never been married. Can't find no woman that could stand to be that happy. I crack myself up. Ain't usually nobody else around. All my partners are somewhere with their wives and kids. I got two, maybe three, knuckleheads scattered around here and there. I take care of my little birds too. Child support eats my ass up every month. But I don't get to see them much, though, on account of their mamas. Ain't found a woman yet that I can get along with for too long.

Back in the day we all hung out on the hill, matter of fact I was the spunk, the pizzazz, you know. Kept the group laughing with my jokes, grabbed myself, tried to rub up against all the pussy I could get next to, and still tried my best to get home early enough to keep the peace with my mama.

When I went up to Kak's house on my own that night, the black and white TV was on but nobody could hear it, nor were they trying to. The TV just added light, like an extra lamp to take the edge off the darkness. I watched the black and white figures dance on the snowy screen for a minute, wishing them old niggas would be quiet so I could hear, but quickly lost interest. My boys were somewhere skating or sitting out on Water Street hill with the girls. I figured they were playing ball, too, but I was at Kak's, getting slapped on the back by brothas old enough to be my father.

"Boy, you all right?" Kak flopped down into a spare space on the couch and the weak springs carried him so low into the seat that I knew he would need help getting up, but I didn't say nothing.

"I'm cool," I said trying to play it off, but Kak could tell I wasn't doing too good.

"You hear Daddy left… moved to Lexington with that woman?"

"Seems to me I did hear something like that. Maxine doing all right?"

"She cries."

"Me and your old man go way back but that don't make him right." Kak lit up a cigarette, blew the smoke up in the air and him and me sat arm to arm, occasionally passing a nod back and forth like men. I didn't say much 'cause I was trying hard, holding back them punk ass tears.

The old timers was cool though, the old regulars, Ramey, Boone, all of them, raised themselves up from their card games and their bullshit sessions and came by to try and cheer me up. Giving me drinks of beer, pressing five-dollar bills into the center of my hand, telling jokes trying to get me to crack a smile. I stayed way past supper, way after my curfew, sipping at a can of beer that I thought tasted like piss.

I was hoping the beer would help make the week bend at the edges, grow fuzzy—but it was still sharp, clear, and all I could think about. The fight had jerked me up out of my sleep. Mama had waited at the door for Daddy to come home. That bitch had called again.

"Gene, I can't take this," Mama screamed, her voice cracking but raising up to levels that I hadn't even heard before. "If you want to choose a whore over your family then choose and get the hell out."

Fussing was nothing new but I could feel it this time, like something swollen and puss-filled that was about to pop. Daddy had tried his regular bullshit, "I don't know what you talking about Maxine. Woman, have you lost your friggin' mind?"

But this time Mama wasn't having it. The phone calls. The notes in his pockets. The all-nighters. The smell of perfume in his clothes.

I knew all about it. I had met the dark-skinned heifer Daddy called Honey. One afternoon we had finished playing basketball up at the school with Daddy jabbing me in the ribs, fouling me left and right. "Where's your defense son?!"

After the game, instead of going home for a shower, Daddy stopped the car in front of that woman's house. I sat glued to her vinyl couch, my shorts soaked with sweat, my scraped knee and bunged up elbow stinging, watching Daddy getting hard from the whispers the woman licked in his ear.

"You are a good-looking boy," she had said to me and bent

down so close to my face that I thought she was going to kiss me. After she brought me a towel and a glass of grape pop, she flipped the TV on and they disappeared upstairs.

"Make yourself at home," she said. "There's bologna in the refrigerator, bread on the counter."

But I sat there not moving the whole time Daddy was upstairs with the woman, who years later would have the nerve to call herself my step mother. I listened to their moans above the cowboy flick playing on the TV. I got up once or twice to turn the television up but I could still hear them. The moaning was new. At home when Mama and Daddy did it, all I could hear was a banging sound. Their headboard tapping out some rhythm against the wall. I bragged a lot about pussy back then but the truth was I had never had any. I wanted to know what the difference was, why Daddy moaned and groaned with her and didn't with my mother. I sat wishing like hell that Mama had followed us there and would come busting through the door any minute. I wanted to go up and peek, but I didn't.

When they came back down, Daddy was tucking his shirt into his blue jean pants and the woman was dressed like before, lipstick and all. The whore looked younger than Mama and even that made me mad.

The woman laughed and kissed Daddy on the cheek. She squatted down beside me and tossed her hair back.

"You sure are a nice looking young man." She winked.

"Look at his old man. Could he help it?" Daddy reared back, shrugged his shoulders and raised his hands up, the way people do when they mean, "What can I say?"

"This is a secret between men," he said and rubbed his knuckles on my head. "What your mama don't know won't hurt her."

As we headed for the door, I set the wet glass on Honey's wooden coffee table and knew what my mama didn't know would be the thing that hurt her the most. But I never told on Daddy. Not once. The son-of-bitch took me there many times. Sometimes he would leave me in the car for hours and return smelling like she smelled, like musk oil. My mother never smelled like that.

I heard Mama that night, tearing into Daddy. A week later I saw the scratches across his face when he came back to the house to get his truck. I didn't know my mother had it in her. Wasn't the right thing to feel, but I felt proud.

"Hit me back you son-of-a-bitch," Mama screamed that night. "I want to see your no good, black ass in jail. Hit me, so I can go right in here and call the law."

"Stop Maxine, I don't hit women," Daddy said. I was waiting, wanting him to get silly and hit Mama just once so I could take my place in the world.

"No, you don't hit women, just fuck all the women you can find. Don't you?"

"Maxine, it's over. Just stop. I'll leave."

In the back of my mind, I pictured the knife shiny and gleaming in the kitchen drawer, a bloody two-by-four in the garage, a smoking gun but then suddenly it was over. I heard a door close. I waited to hear it open up again. Waited to hear him at least come back and say good-bye to me, but he never did.

The next morning, when I went to the kitchen for breakfast, Mama seated me in Daddy's chair. She scampered around the table, filling up my juice glass and my milk glass and shoveled Daddy's portion of the scrambled eggs onto my plate. She tried to smile, tried to hum like she always did but I could see something wrenching at her guts. We ate breakfast and hardly said two words. Mama stared at me and whenever I made a move to get up for something, she second guessed me and ran to get the butter, the jelly, the salt, the pepper, a paper towel, more toast, until I said, "I'm full Mama. I'm fine."

The sound of my words broke the silence and Mama cried like a baby, slumped out of her chair and slid to the floor and cried. She lay on the cold linoleum, her dress hiked up around her thighs, her body folded up like she had a bellyache.

"Come on Mama, now. He ain't worth it. Don't cry." I wondered if I should have told.

Mama cried like she was grieving over somebody dead,

choking and grabbing for air in her lungs. I went over and put my arms around her like I was her daddy and tried to get her up off the floor. When we finally stood up, Mama held me close and tight and wouldn't let go. I loved her, but I felt smothered like she had gone crazy. Like maybe she wouldn't ever let me go.

"You know you the man of the house now," she said. "Please don't turn out like that son-of-a-bitch. Please don't."

My mother spun me around by the shoulders, suddenly she was my mother again. She shook me like I was ten years old and had just ran out in front of a car or something just as dangerous.

"Promise me you won't."

"You hurtin my arms Mama."

"If you turn out like that son-of-bitch, I swear to God, I'll kill you myself." She slapped me hard. "Do you hear me son?!"

"Yes, ma'am."

That was at least one moment in my life when I knew my mother was in full charge, no matter if I thought I was growing up or not. I was scared to death and worried. I had never seen my mother like this.

She burnt all of Daddy's clothes in the back yard. I watched her from the kitchen. Saw the circle of his hats, shirts, dungarees and shoes go up in flames, then char down to smoke and coals, a new hard look in her eyes that remains to this day. I listened to Mama crying up in the night. I both wanted to comfort her and to get as far away from her as I could.

A big part of me was glad Daddy was gone. I was sick and tired of his bullshit but I still waited for a phone call or a visit. Something. Eventually he came around now and then to see me, or I'd run into him in the streets.

"What's up, man?" he'd say like I was just another brotha on the street and not his flesh and blood. He would slap me a five, hit me in the shoulder and keep on stepping. Some daddy I had.

Mama begged me that morning to not be like my father but I think I'm his twin. It's hard to know for sure. Sometimes I think I'm just like him.

It would be years after that night he left, before me and Daddy, all quiet and looking like a younger and older version of the same man, made some kind of peace, shaking each other's hands and posing for a picture at a family reunion.

"Son, I ain't never been perfect," he said to me just out of the blue like that.

"Me neither," I said. Wasn't much but all we could get from each other and both of us walked away with tears in our eyes. Even then I didn't forgive his old ass. Not completely.

I try to keep focused on the positive, on our little truce, but mostly my mind floats back to that night after he left. That first night at Kak's—the night I drank my first beers. I was still there after all the men had gotten drunk and staggered their way back home. I knew Mama was gonna be mad or be worried, that she'd probably whip my ass good, but that night I didn't care. I kept my crack planted on Kak's couch, trying my man pants on for size.

The Evolution of Sandy Crawford

Sandy

The Evolution of Sandy Crawford

It was 4 A.M. and Sandy Crawford had just finished pressing and rolling her hair. Even with the air-conditioner blasting, tiny clumps of hair were already beading up around her ears. Watching her hair fighting it's way back to its natural state right before her eyes made her think of her cousin, Jacinda, who had showed up at the reunion a few years back with her head slicked clean like a man's. The next year Jacinda had little plaits all over her head and had wrapped it in a psychedelic scarf. Sandy and all the other Crawford women had stared and had shaken their heads.

"Look at that child, a hippie. A bona fide Aunt Jemima hippie shore nuff." Couldn't help herself.

"Go natural, sisters!" Jacinda retorted, her hair wiggling out like tiny wild snakes from beneath the scarf.

To Sandy the year Jacinda arrived with African jewelry all over her hands, neck, wrists, nose, even on her ankles, and tried to convince them all that her new name was Yoruba—took the cake. Yoruba Crawford. Now ain't that a mess.

The only thing good about it was that Jacinda had brought

a nice-looking young man with her. Right smart young fellow but he was a tall chocolate fellow showing up in their butterscotch family—his hair, like rope, down to his waist. He didn't eat this, didn't drink that, but he had Crawford women clamoring to wait on him hand and foot all day.

Sandy smiled at what was to come. For sure it would be chaos but worth every bit. Maybe Reverend Townsend would stop by. He loved her cooking.

In the mirror she saw her mother's face and still hadn't gotten use to that idea. A husband, two kids, chin hairs and, could that be a wrinkle? She was up working, while the rest of her house leisured their carefree asses in their beds, but there was a part of this she liked. She took a breath, one deep cleansing breath, like the woman on the meditation tape had said. Jacinda had sent the tape for Christmas (even though she had said it was for Kwanzaa). Then, deep mindful breathing until she reached her center, the meditation woman had said. Sandy closed her eyes and took several shallow breaths. She felt silly and glad that Norman and the kids were asleep and couldn't see her nonsense.

"Okay, enough of that," she said louder than she meant to. "I've got work to do."

Time to check on the greens she had stewing on the stove, the turkey she had in the oven. She needed to see if the cake had cooled enough to receive icing. Sandy took one last look at herself in the mirror, accidentally flipping the mirror to the magnified side.

"Oh, Lord," she said to herself. "Forty-five and counting."

Company was coming soon. In less than six hours, Sandy's house, which she had spent the night cleaning from top to bottom, would be flooded with relatives. The first year she and Norman had hosted the Crawford family reunion it had been her idea. All she had really wanted to do was show off the new addition of a family room in the back and the remodeled patio, complete with a turf rug, a water foundation, which had cost Norman a fortune, and all the tropical plants that one room could hold. But now, five years later, it never failed that in the winter, usually after Christmas, relatives from Kentucky to California would start calling to see if they had set the July date yet.

In the kitchen, Sandy removed the top from the cafeteria-sized pan of mustard greens. The smell of down-home food always reminded her of when she was a young girl growing up in the country. How she missed her mother at times like this. Beside the large pan, on the smaller burner, was the vegetarian version of the greens. Some members of the family had become healthier. *Hummmp,* Sandy thought, if she could ever escape Norman's same-old, same-old then maybe she would become pork- and beef-free too. Maybe she'd even "go natural" with Jacinda. Her laughter echoed off the cabinets.

She could see Norman with his hands resting on his belly, looking six months along, gaping at her baldhead sideways and wanting to know where his pork chops were.

Out the window, beyond the patio, in her backyard, Sandy could see from the streetlight that her tomatoes needed to be picked; even from where she stood she saw some of the swollen, red fruits straining the vines. She'd have to get them before those badass kids in the neighborhood got to them.

Sandy's kitchen was tiny, compared to most, but she was in arm's reach of everything. She'd need a larger one if she continued to entertain. Had she remembered everything? Macaroni and cheese; baked beans, one with pork bacon, one with turkey drippings; potato salad; macaroni salad; *salad* salad with French dressing, the only way Uncle Fred liked it; blackberry cobbler; peach cobbler; the 7-UP cake still cooling on the counter; potato chips and Kool-Aid for the kids; organic apple juice for Jacinda; TAB pop for the ones with sugar; the yeast rolls were rising for the second time. Damn—the turkey. Sandy reached behind the stove and pulled the potholder off the wall and rescued the slow-cooked turkey with precision. She rubbed the drippings that splashed on her arms, on her apron. The yeast rolls had to rise one more time.

Sandy plopped herself into one of the dinette chairs and cradled her head in her hand. Checked her egg-splattered list one more time. This was her last year doing this. Next year she was going to be luxuriating in somebody else's yard or there would be no Crawford Family Reunion. But who could possibly do this like her?

Sandy loved her family but sometimes she mourned for her girl-self—being tucked in by her mother, a book in her hand, and a stuffed animal by her side, the country breeze blowing in her open window.

She remembered the Norman she had met in church, tall, bony, good looking. Back then she had been the shy one. It was Norman who had walked right up on her one Easter. His words still hung fresh in her ears, "You are the finest thing walking," which was a bold-faced lie but good to hear. Sandy got tickled thinking about her teenaged self. She was just as skinny as Norman, so scrawny her mama had called her 'Chicken Little.' Legs like ravelings, long black threads. Norman was fire back then and the littlest of his mama's boys, straight up like a light pole. The other Jackson boys were beefy, wide shoulders, muscular torsos. Sandy and Norman had gone from courting to married in fourteen days and it had lasted all these years. She could see them now, standing at the altar up like two pole beans, long-armed and goofy in love. She recalled her wedding dress—sky blue with an A-line skirt—and its tiny, tiny waist. Sandy patted her round belly and jiggled the loose fat on her arm.

"Time sure done moved on," she said to the quiet, and smiled.

And times had changed sure enough. Sandy was the loud one now and Norman's spirit had quieted down. But she sometimes wished Norman would get bold again, take charge; and she missed her peaceful self.

On this morning Sandy was remembering everything. She remembered the kids when they were real little. The days when they laid around on Saturday mornings watching cartoons, waiting on her to cook a big Saturday breakfast—scrambled eggs, country ham, biscuits, gravy and fresh-squeezed orange juice.

By the time the first of the Crawfords arrived, Sandy had fixed her hair into a lightly-picked froth of curls, put on her new flowered shorts outfit and dabbed on a little lipstick, stylish but not too young for her age. Norman and the kids had gobbled up their breakfast and she had washed the dishes hours ago. She left them to dress themselves. It was the least they could do although she was frightened of what they might pick out. The cake was iced with her lemon-rind butter frosting and everything was on the patio laid out on top of the long, portable tables she had finally got Norman to pull from the garage just an hour before.

"Sandy, one table is enough," he had argued, "this is family we're talking about, you ain't receiving no company for real, just family." Then he had given in, had become suddenly quiet. He plopped the table down and started helping her put the food on it, almost before she even got a chance to wipe it down and put her new tablecloth in place. She smoothed a wrinkle in the corner of the bright blue cloth and rearranged the matching serving bowls, napkins and tumbler set. Norman was incapable of placing anything to her suiting. And what in the hell was he wearing? A yellow golf shirt with green slacks. He was totally mismatched and wrinkled but Sandy bit her tongue and kept on working.

Everyone who came in greeted Sandy with a sloppy kiss. Cousins, aunts, uncles, sisters, lots and lots of kids. Crawfords galore. She smiled her polite smile. Not the fake one she used in church and at work, but the one she saved up all year for her family. The smile she mostly gave to those who passed through the patio and shouted, "Oh, my goodness Sandy, you've outdone yourself again!"

By 3 P.M. Sandy's nerves were frazzled, the kids, who ran through her house like wild horses, had drunk all the Kool-Aid, the bit that wasn't spilled all over the house; somebody had forked a chunk out of her 7-UP cake before dinner; and her rolls, which she had trusted one of her aunts to watch, were black on the bottom. Any Crawford woman worth her salt would have the sense to know when yeast rolls were done. She tried to take another cleansing breath but it wasn't cleansing anything.

Norman had just gotten everyone's attention and the house, although filled with more than twenty people, was quieter than it had been all day. Uncle Fred came forward to say the blessing. Except for a baby crying somewhere in the house, everything was peaceful. Sandy thought she could get used to this. Uncle Fred prayed, his voice rising and falling like an old time spiritual. Sandy was reveling in the moment, riding on Uncle Fred's voice like a fresh breeze, when the doorbell rang. Before anyone could answer the door, a distant uncle, who Sandy instantly and intuitively knew had descended from one of the bad sides, toppled through the door, a wet spot rising in the front of his lime-green pants, his hat toppling off his head, his eyes bloodshot and bulging, smelling of cigar smoke, sweat and the strongest of liquor. Sandy hoped none of the neighbors had seen him. She prayed that Reverend Townsend would stay home.

"I love my fucking family," he screamed, his speech slurring, drawing the curse word out long and forever. The children in earshot covered their mouths in disbelief. "God bless all y'all. Look what God done did for us. All this right here. The Lord made a way for us!" The drunk cousin waved his hands around and began to cry. Opened his arms for a hug.

"Come here, Sandy, and give your cuz a kiss. Lord, I ain't seen you in years! Look just like yo mama for the world. Margaret Jean made over. Yes, suh."

Sandy turned her back to the teetering little man as Norman and another cousin swooped in just in time to catch him before he hit the floor. She wanted to say that he wasn't a relative and wished Norman would just put him out but somewhere in his little drunk face she recognized someone she had met before: Aunt Hettie's boy, she thought… The nerve. Why couldn't he have stayed under the creek rock he had crawled out from under?

From the corner of her eye, Sandy caught sight of her twelve year old daughter, who hadn't made an appearance all day, descending from the steps, wearing blue jean cut offs that barely left material for the crotch, a midriff blouse that extended up showing her bra, and sunglasses the color of ripe lemons. Sandy's son followed behind her, looking wrinkled but normal. Thank God for small favors. In the distance—which she wished was miles away—Sandy heard her glass punch bowl, which had held the Kool-Aid, crashing to the patio floor. She closed her eyes. Breathe. In. Breathe. Out. Breathe in. Breathe out. She was starting to feel better. BreatheinBreatheout. Inout.Inout.

When Sandy came to in her own bed, Jacinda was standing over her, her long ropy dreadlocks pulled back in a fashionable ponytail. Sandy had hyperventilated. From a distance, down the stairs and through the front hall, through the kitchen and onto the patio, she could hear the Crawford Reunion continuing without her. She was glad she had passed out before she could fully witness Norman and Cousin Walter Senior placing the pissy cousin on her nice sofa. Just the thought of it made her feel faint even now. Norman peeped into the bedroom door, allowing in more noise than Sandy could tolerate all at once.

"Norman, go tell your daughter to put some clothes on her tail," she mustered.

"She okay?" Norman nodded toward Sandy as though she was still unconscious.

"She's fine," Jacinda said before Norman hurried back out the door.

Jacinda and Sandy visited a long time. At first Sandy was resistant to Jacinda's gobbledy-gook talk of spiritual quests, journeys of the mind, transcendental therapy, self-preservation, relaxation and self-love. Sandy didn't have a clue what half the shit was that Jacinda was talking about, but it sounded good. Sounded like ocean. So she stayed there deep in the pillow like a child hearing a bedtime story and listened.

"You need to get in touch with your spirit," Jacinda said to Sandy, scribbling numerals and letters on a notebook then stopping and studying what she had written. From her purse she pulled out a deck of cards and shuffled them across the edge of the bed and consulted a book with bent and frayed edges. Something she had obviously looked at many times.

"Uh huh," Jacinda muttered under her breath. "Just what I thought."

"What in the hell are you doing, Jacinda?" Sandy asked, raising herself up off the pillows. "You gonna send me straight to hell in my own house. Put that shit up! God's watching you, Jacinda."

"Seems like you the one he needs to have his eye on."

"Crazy heifer," Sandy muttered under her breath.

But Sandy began to relax when Jacinda began massaging her temples before she caught herself and jerked up again. In the quiet, Jacinda moved her long fingers along the sides of her cousin's face and along the sides of her neck where the tension rose up in knots along her shoulders. Sandy closed her eyes.

Jacinda removed a small package of incense from her purse, struck a match to it and began moving the smoking stick through the air. Thick sweet lavender smoke filled the room. She continued the massage.

"Girl, get your hands off me. You gonna burn my fucking house down. I'll be damned."

Sandy sat full up on the edge of the bed.

"Okay," Jacinda said blowing out the incense and shaking her head. "But you need something."

"And you need Jesus."

Sandy closed her eyes again and prayed for God to deliver her. Not the incense breathing, meditating, massaging-God that Jacinda had brought into the room with her, but just the plain old regular Baptist God that she was used to.

"Take care of you," Jacinda said as she stood up, drawing out the *you.* "Ain't nobody gonna do it if you don't." Jacinda kissed Sandy's forehead.

"What would Aunt Margaret say?" She whispered.

"I don't know," Sandy said, furious that Jacinda would bring up her dead mother. "But I have a headache and if you don't mind I would like to get some rest."

"Love you," Jacinda threw back over her shoulder.

"Love you, too, now take your ass on."

Sandy shooed Jacinda out of the bedroom and smiled to herself. She really did love Jacinda with her crazy self. She'd try to spend more time with her tomorrow, after she got this mess cleaned up.

Sandy placed the cool, wet, washcloth over the headache that was throbbing over her left eye. A stroke, she thought to herself. There is a stroke forming in my head right now. This is too much. What *would* Mama say? What would she think of all this? What would she think of me? Here she was the daughter of down-to-earth people trying to present herself as high sidity—the royal queen of Water Street, with her highfalutin house and furniture. Perfection. Her head throbbed even more and the pain seemed to bore a hole in the center of her eyeball when she thought of her parents quietly sharing a meal at the dinner table. Content in their simple life.

Sandy couldn't bring herself to get up and say goodbye to her company. She could hear the front door opening and closing. She heard the out-of-town Crawfords, who would be spending the night, settling themselves in the spare room. She didn't have the energy to get up and show them where she kept the clean towels, to tell them what time she would have breakfast ready or to stay up all night talking about 'remember whens.' And this was so unlike her.

At some point in the night, she heard the teenagers from the neighborhood out on the hill. She couldn't make out what they were saying or who was saying what but the youthfulness in their voices strangely calmed her this time. She lay there with her eyes closed and tried to picture them laughing and talking, sitting in a circle. She could see the Patton girls cutting their eyes at one of the boys, Junior, maybe. She could hear the elevated squeal of Yolanda's laughter, the response of Mouse's jokes. In her own mind she could even see the Stokes girl up against the car with one of them no-count bushy headed boys but she didn't have the strength to make it to the window to seek out the particulars. Even the music they played didn't seem to be getting on her nerves. Before this night she had been known for raising her window and shooing them all back down the street, or calling their parents and accusing them of not supervising their children properly. But this time she was preoccupied. Where had the years gone?

At 3 A.M. Sandy awakened. She left Norman sleeping in the bed and tiptoed downstairs. Her plastic parrot cups and plates were strewn all through the house. Swallows of Kool-Aid, apple juice, beer, left in the cups. Some of the plates were still piled high with potato salad or beans or greens. On almost every plate there was a lone yeast roll, one bite taken from it; even worse were the rolls that lay abandoned, with their black sides facing upward.

In the kitchen it was clear that not a soul had noticed the extra parrot dishes under the patio table: her sink was piled window-high with dishes from her cabinet. Sandy almost collapsed to see that someone even used her wedding china. All the pots and pans were near empty; a turkey carcass was still in the center of her kitchen table.

Sandy made her way past the mess on the patio, into the backyard, then beyond the clothesline to the tomato vines that edged the garden. She bit into the first tomato she saw. It was red, firm and warm as the July sun, so large it had begun to split from its middle. Sandy bit again and remembered doing this as a child, on summer nights the sky was lit up by the full moon's big eye and the quiet came sprinkled only with the noises that creatures that live close to the dirt make. Back over Sandy's left shoulder, the house she had abandoned in the middle of the night was dark, except for the porch light. There on the ground in the tomato patch she sat, insects crawling on her thighs and ankles.

Under a moonlit summer morning, she sat eating tomatoes off the vine, juice running down her chin. There she was, her sweaty hips planted in between rows of tomatoes, her breath moving in and out with the flare of each nostril. Her eyes closed. A light wind tickled her arms—making the hair rise up on end. She heard the silence broken by the clacking of the back door. She heard Norman's voice.

"Sandy, Sandy," he yelled, "Where are you?"

Between the sticks and the tomato vines, Sandy could see her son and daughter joining their father circled together at the back steps. Even from where she crouched on the ground, she could hear the panic rising in Norman's voice.

"Sandy!"

His voice made the insects scatter, made the night creatures stir.

"Mama," her daughter chimed in followed by her brother.

"This don't make no sense."

Soon the other Crawfords joined them.

"Where could she be?" she heard one of them ask. "Do you think something has happened?"

"Should we call the law?" another asked.

By then her sassy daughter's voice had turned into her little girl again.

"Mama! Mama!"

"Daddy, where is Mama at?"

Sandy closed her eyes, tousled her hair. She took another cleansing breath, began her deep breathing. The next time she heard Norman he sounded on the edge of panic, his voice rising up strong and loud. Sandy stayed quiet, stayed low to the sweet ground. The Crawfords drew closer. Sandy could hear the swish of the grass, could feel her hair coiling up on her head, going from straight to nappy in the heat. As her family crept up on her, their faces popping up in the garden one by one, the first red sky of morning was peeking up over Water Street and the grandest reaction Sandy Crawford could muster was a wide, girlish smile.

The Girl of my Dreams

Kiki

The Girl of my Dreams

The night before my wedding the child comes to me again. She's wearing a diaper and a T-shirt. A light-skinned little girl, looking just like me. She hollers out, "Daddy! Daddy!" Her pigtails flying. She's going through that stage where her two teeth seem to be the biggest thing about her. She doesn't smile but she's pretty; looks just like Ina.

I think about her all the time, not Ina so much anymore, but the little girl I think we made. She shows up in my dreams, in church with her new parents. I see her among any group of young girls, her head cocked to the side like Yolanda, my sister. Every time I see a little girl, I take a second look. I don't even know why I'm convinced that the child is a girl. I just am.

When somebody asks me, "Do you have any kids?" I say, "Not that I know of." It's an old joke. Everybody laughs, but it's true. I don't know for sure. At night when I'm lying in bed, it's not funny to me at all then. This child is a stubborn soul. She's always somewhere in the back of my mind.

I have opened my mouth to tell Nadine, my fiancé, many

times about the possibilities of this child but I can never find the words. "What is it Kevin?" she asks sometimes when I'm staring out into the world but I always pull her close and kiss her, "I love you," I say but deep down I'm not sure if I want to marry Nadine. I don't know if I'm ready.

Nadine refuses to call me Kiki like the rest of my family. Her family is not the type to do such things. I don't recall her mother smiling once. She is the saddest woman I've ever seen. I look at her and hope I don't see my future. Nadine's mother is always dressed up, even late on Friday nights and on lazy Saturday mornings. I have never seen her without stockings, without a dress, without make-up, without jewelry. My future father-in-law is the same way. It is as though they are cardboard cutouts positioned in the perfect house, with the perfect family: one daughter, one son, a small Chihuahua for effect, and a future son-in-law to mix things up a bit. Nadine and her mother have planned this huge wedding to the tune of ten thousand dollars. Although I'm not paying for it, I look at Nadine's parents and know these are not the type of people I want to be indebted to.

I met Nadine at the bookstore in Danville. I am not the smartest cat but I read every now and then. Somebody at work had said I should read Richard Wright's *Black Boy* so I was getting them to order it for me. I already had the tiny shelf over my bed filled with James Baldwin, Langston Hughes, Leroi Jones and Samuel Delaney. I also had a little Stephen King, Sherlock Holmes and George Orwell thrown in too. I've always been a reader but they never let us read those kinds of books in school. When I saw Nadine I knew she was not the type of woman who would give out her phone number easily, so I saw it as a challenge. Six months later we were in love.

I love Nadine, but she is the type of woman who puts a towel down before sex, strips off the bed afterwards, and insists that I brush my teeth every time I go down on her. I know she is the type of wife who will only give me oral sex on birthdays, Valentine's Day and our anniversary. We will eat with the in-laws in fine restaurants. She will look good on my arm when I make it to the top. Our children will be clean all the time and she will nag me if I leave my underwear on the bathroom floor. I know these things already. They are not things that I've ever thought about before but on the eve of my wedding they are all I can think about.

Ina was gorgeous. A college sophomore from Indianapolis. I remember there was always something stuck-up about Ina, too, but I liked that. Maybe that is just the type of woman I like. Ina wasn't like the other girls I knew. I met her in the mall. I was coming out of the record store and she was on her way in. I caught her looking at the new Rick James album.

"If you want it, it's yours," I said cool as ice. Just like that.

"What?!" Ina was startled but began to laugh.

"Can't you come with better rap than that, brother?"

We both laughed and we went from there. I drove up to Lexington to see her every weekend in my seventy-two Impala. Mean green, bad as she wanted to be. When Ina came to Stanford to see me, I walked her all over town, so the hometown folks could see what kind of fish I caught.

I met Ina's parents once when they came down to visit her at the dorm in Lexington. They looked me up and down like I was trash. Her daddy talked like that Thurston cat on *Gilligan's Island* and looked at me like I was there to shine his shoes. Her mama had that air, too, like she thought her shit didn't stink. Maybe I'm just drawn to these types of people.

Ina was more down to earth but she couldn't help herself sometimes. She thought I was country, not that Indianapolis was all that it was cracked up to be. She said it wasn't about nothing either. Sometimes she talked over my head when she began talking her college stuff. I guess I could have went to college too but I didn't, so when I didn't have a clue as to what she was talking about, I just said, "Dig, dig," like I understood it all. But I knew I didn't.

Ina called me out of the blue one night, her voice quivering like something was wrong.

"You're what?" That's about all I could say. Pregnant. I couldn't do much but just hold the phone and listen.

My head was fogged up. It was all happening too fast for me to catch up. I wanted to say *It ain't mine* like I had seen brothers I hung with do in that kind of predicament but I knew it probably *was* mine. I couldn't ask her to marry me, because that was too deep. We'd only been going together for eight months so I just hung on the phone, listening to her voice. For minutes we listened to each other breathe.

"Kiki, you hear me? You still there?"

"Uh-huh."

"They want me to go away then have the baby and put it up for adoption."

"What? That sounds like some bourgeois shit. Don't nobody do that. I know girls with babies. Wait a minute, Ina. I'll help you out. I'll be a man."

"They said, *No*, Kiki."

"Girl you twenty years old…" I don't know why I panicked. It wasn't like at twenty-five I was ready for a baby but I had to say something so she knew I cared.

"I've got to finish school." She started crying.

"Do you think we should get an abortion?" I felt bad about that one as soon as it came out of my mouth.

"We? Kiki there ain't no *we* if that's all you got to say." The phone went to a dial tone. I guess that at a time like that nothing I said would have been the right thing. I tried to call back for a few days but all I got was a busy signal. When I finally got through a week later, Ina's roommate answered the phone.

"She's gone."

"Gone?! What do you mean she's gone?"

"G-o-n-e. Packed up moved out. Her parents came and picked her up."

"Is there a phone number?"

"No."

If I said I'd tried hard to find her or to find out what

happened I would be lying. My mama and daddy don't know about this. My sister doesn't know either. Hell, even I don't know. I could have made it up to Indianapolis and searched the place but I'm sure that even if I had found them, Ina's mother and father would have never let me see her.

I watch other men with their children and wonder what kind of father I would have been. I wonder if Ina and me would have gotten along. I've been with a whole string of women since Ina but I don't have any other kids because I'm careful. One scare is enough.

I watched Nadine tonight at the rehearsal dinner and I can't picture her as a mother. I know she will be the mother of my children but I can't imagine her large stomach or a waddling behind. I can't see her cleaning up baby vomit or poop. I smile at the thought of her in her nice clothes, folding up a dirty diaper.

It's a pivotal moment in your life when you look out down the table at your wedding rehearsal dinner and realize that you have been to bed with nearly every woman who will attend your wedding.

Trudy, my brother-in-law's girlfriend, was the first girl I ever messed with.

Mona, my sister's best friend, is one I'm still ashamed of. She was too young and I knew it but couldn't help myself at the time.

Athena, who works for the catering service: We did it one night after a party. She winks at me as she spoons gravy over the roast beef on each dinner guest's plate.

Josephine will be here tomorrow from Chattanooga, a high school sweetheart.

And lots more. Who knows what to expect tomorrow?

The fathers, both Nadine's and mine, make a toast to the bride and groom. I eat and smile through the whole thing, but my mind is lost.

"Kevin, Sweetie?" Nadine loops her arm into mine, "I want to introduce you to someone." It is one of her little cousins; a beautiful girl, about the age my daughter would be. "This is Kevin," she says. "Kevin, this is Amie."

The little girl snuggles up against Nadine. "Watch Cousin

Nadine's dress, baby," Nadine says and hugs the child at arm's length. The girl looks at me and grins a shy smile. She removes her finger from her mouth and waves at me with it before she runs back to her mother.

Maybe my ghost girl was jealous because she came into my mind at that moment and has stayed. After the rehearsal dinner, I took a nap to rest up for the bachelor party. In my dreams the photographer snaps the pictures and when they come back Nadine wants to know who this child in the yellow dress is in every picture. I try to explain to her that she's my daughter, but Nadine, of course, doesn't understand. She cries and says that I have betrayed her. My daughter giggles and plays ring-around-the-rosie with Amie, around and around and around.

Ray Ray, Kenny and Meaty come knocking on the door of my apartment at nine. They have brought me spirits—a massive amount of liquor to drown my bachelor blues in. Even though I've always thought we would be the type of gang who would have bachelor parties with hookers and strippers, my bachelor party is a drinking-walk-down-memory-lane-remember-when-type of affair. By ten o'clock I am drunk on my ass.

"Kiki remember that time we fucked them girls right out in the open, under the bleachers at the football game. Fucking thirty degrees almost froze my nuts off." Meaty is pissy drunk and leaning on Kenny, laughing so hard he can barely get it out.

"Yeah, man," I say and shake my head, trying to shake off the memory. "And remember that *you* was scared that the teachers almost busted us when they came around back to gather up the smokers." We are all laughing so hard that we are all holding on to our sides. Nothing that is being said is that funny and it's even more than that. In some ways I think we are trying to reclaim our childhoods for the last time.

"Miss Sandy," Ray Ray begins. And we all take a deep breath and break out into a roaring laugh before he gets any further. "That woman wanted to whip our asses so bad. Now why in the world did we get on that woman's nerves so bad? We ought have been ashamed of our little bad asses."

"But we wasn't!" Kenny screams and plants high fives all around the circle.

We laugh like waves. A big one crashes through, then ripples down to silence, before somebody else brings up some other past craziness that we did as boys.

At some later moment, when we are full of liquor and stories and have began a friendly game of spades, the phone rings. It is Yolanda, my sister. Hearing her voice reminds me of when we were little.

"Hey Pudge," I say.

"Yolanda," she says, but I hear a sadness in her voice.

"What's wrong Pudge?" This time she buys it and doesn't correct me. She just starts talking.

"Just calling. My big brother is tying the knot tomorrow, huh?"

"Yep."

"Well I hope she knows she's marrying the most hard headed, meanest, most rotten son-of-a-bitch this side of Lexington."

"Corny."

Yolanda laughs but I hear something more serious in her voice. I can sense that her husband, Junior, is there and she can't get too far into it, so I try to talk it out with her from my side.

"Junior messing around on you again?"

"Not sure."

"You think so?"

"Not sure."

"Feeling depressed again, Yo?"

There is no answer on the end of the phone.

"You sick again, Pudge?"

"I hope not," she finally answers but I hear the doubt in her voice. My sister is having depression again. It comes on her like great waves. She can be happy as a lark then suddenly plummet so low that she stays in bed for weeks. She's the nervous type. Doesn't take much to set her off.

"I hope not either, Pudge. Have you talked to Junior?"

"No."

"Mama?"

"No."

"The doctor?"

"Sorta."

I just hold the phone and know that before I go to bed I will have to call my mother and tell her that her daughter is spiraling again. We all go through this every few months. I wonder for a minute how Nadine will adjust to my sister's condition. She seems to like her all right, but this is another thing that she doesn't know.

"Pudge take your medicine and try to get some sleep. We've all got a big day tomorrow. You sure Junior's there?"

"Yes, he is, Kiki." I hate when she answers me like she's angry with me because I just treated her like a child. I hear Junior and her daughter, Shauna, talking in the background.

"I love you Pudge, Pudge, Pudge." I had to say it even if the fellows look at me and laugh.

"Tell them to kiss my ass," my sister says before she tells me she loves me back and hangs up the phone. I am relieved that she laughed at the end, laughing is always a good sign.

It is well past midnight when the brothas leave and by then my apartment is filled with half empty beer cans and bottles of liquor. Potato chip dip is spoiling in the heat. They have been so loud that it takes a moment to adjust to the quiet when I shut the door behind them.

I pick up the phone to call my mother and really figure it's late to be calling but I need to hear her voice anyway, so I dial. My father picks up on the first ring.

"Daddy, is Mama still up?"

"We both are son." Before I've had a chance to apologize, he has passed the phone.

I tell my mother that Yolanda is feeling bad again. I hear my mother sigh at the other end of the line. It is a deep, long sigh and I wonder what that must feel like, to be the parent of a sick child. To hurt so much from someone else's pain.

In the end my mother says, "Cheer up baby, it's all gonna work itself out. Tomorrow's your big day. My baby is getting himself hitched." I can hear the lilt in my mother's voice and I want to cry out to her and tell her that her baby also has a baby. That her baby is not sure if he wants to be hitched.

When I get off the phone I think of my parents' perfect marriage—the way Daddy would smile at Mama right before we were ran off to bed. The family car washes in the driveway. I think of me teasing Pudgie like crazy when we were little—burying her Barbie dolls and stepping through her pretend castles; and I think of my child again. This time I am not even sure she is Ina's child but she is a woman's child that I love. We are a real family like mine, three smiling faces on the couch—my arm crooked around my wife, the child leaning sleepily into her mother. I try hard to make Nadine fit into the body of my wife but she will not enter the dream. I cannot make it so.

Alone in the dark, I think of Nadine. I try to imagine myself telling her about all my past girlfriends and her laughing. I try to imagine myself telling her about my sister and her being sympathetic and caring. I think of myself telling her about my child and her agreeing to search the ends of the earth until we find her. But in reality I know that in those situations Nadine would go from anger to silence and back to anger. She would think that I am a failure, my sister crazy and maybe even say that those things would never happen in her own family.

It is going on two o'clock when I call Nadine. She answers the phone innocently with sleep still drifting through her voice.

"Baby," she says to me in a playful voice, "are you drunk? It's two in the morning."

"Not any more," I say.

"Were there hookers?"

"No."

"What's wrong? You sound so down. Today is the happiest day of our lives."

"I'm just tired, that's all. I need to get some sleep."

Nadine is silent for a moment then speaks into the phone, her voice careful and a bit unsure. "Then you need to get some sleep then. So you can be fresh by five."

"Kiss, kiss," she says into the phone and waits for my response.

"Kiss, kiss" she repeats again until I answer.

"Hug, hug."

I stop Nadine before she hangs up the phone and I have to blurt it out before I change my mind. "We need to talk," I say, "I've got too many problems right now."

"Kevin, you are just tired, now just go to sleep and I'll see you at the church..."

I waited, hoping she would say: What problems? That she would say: Baby, I'm here for you, I'll be right over. But she says, "You must be out of your fucking mind. My whole damn family is going to be at that church."

"We just need to talk."

In the next few minutes Nadine's screaming is so riddled with herself and what I am doing to her—nothing about me—that I say good-bye to her and hang up the phone. As I place the phone on its cradle, I hear Nadine crying like a wounded child. This makes me sick to my stomach and I hope I'm doing the right thing. I hang up the phone, thinking that when the sun comes up I will call her back and apologize. I will tell her that my daughter has sent for me and I cannot fail her again.

Spoiled

Maxine

Spoiled

Maxine Mason heard someone say once that mothers spoil their sons and raise their daughters. She turned that thought around and around in her head like that spinning wheel at the county fair, but she had never birthed daughters. Mouse was her only child. Still warm from the dryer, she folded Mouse's blue jeans... She smelled them, ran her cheek up and down the leg of the denim, folded his sports shirts, careful to turn down the collars. It was something she had done even when his clothes were much smaller. She had found herself fascinated with the tiny tennis shoes, the pastel terry cloth snap-ups that came in colors that reminded her of Easter. The fuzzy blue snowsuit that she bundled him in the day he came home from the hospital. He had been hot and sweaty when she unzipped him. The snowsuit had been too much for September. Could a mother ever do *too much?*

You're always fussing over him. Let him walk, Maxine. Put him down. Tie the boy's shoes? Hell, he's ten years old! When's he gonna learn to tie his own damn shoes?

She remembers Mouse's tiny, brown feet the day of his birth. How his feet and his hands were the only brown parts of him. He had been premature and so small that Maxine could nearly hold him in one hand. Five pounds, three ounces. His skin was wrinkled those first few days, looking just like a mouse. He was named Monte after Eugene's father but the nickname stuck all these years.

Eugene's sister, Cookie, stood over Maxine's hospital bed, two thick braids snaking down and back on either side of her head. Flailing arms, bracelets clanging and bright yellow dress flashing like a caution signal all over the room.

"That ain't Gene's baby! That baby don't look nothing like my brother! Not one thing on him. That baby's got a white daddy somewhere."

Her loud, red mouth focusing on Maxine with all its fury.

But at the moment she held her son in her arms and looked into his eyes, Maxine was in love. Not a romantic love, but almost. It hadn't mattered that Gene acted a fool. That he accused her of lying down with some white man just because his crazy sister said so. Now she wondered if all the accusations had come from his own guilt. Maybe he was messing around even then. It hadn't mattered that it took the boy two months to turn the color of the dark beer his daddy drank on Saturday nights.

It was what Maxine sensed behind those little eyes on that first day that mattered: that knowing thing that had started between them even before he was born. The moment she knew that it was a little miracle forming in her belly. The moment Mouse was born, Maxine knew her baby recognized her as being someone who belonged to him for life. It was a hushed pact between them. A vow of sorts. Something she thought would always be. But that was before this new space opened up. Before the unraveling started. Before this new thing threatened to swallow her whole.

"That boy can't fix his own supper plate. A damn shame. You done spoiled him. Rotten to the core. Ain't never gonna be no count to nobody. Some kinda mama's boy fool his whole damn life."

Gene had always been jealous of the looks that crossed between

Maxine and Mouse. Knew from day one that a big part of his woman was gone forever. Knew he could never compete with her mothering no matter how hard he tried. A thread had already been pulled.

Before the baby came things had been different.

Baby, can you wear the orange sweater? I like to see you in that.

Every time they headed out to dinner or to a dance Gene would ask her to wear special things for him. They had never had a marriage filled with negligees or sexy frills but there had been something alive there once. Sometimes Maxine would be sitting in the living room reading a book, naked from the waist down, wearing only one of Gene's favorite bras or one of his T-shirts. The memory of legs locked, Gene's hands moving across her, tweaked some dormant feeling buried beneath her maternal self, but she stuffed it back in neat, tidy, like a starched white blouse being tucked into a skirt. That was before the phone started ringing in the middle of the night, before Gene came home late smelling of perfume with lie after lie after lie. Maxine rested her elbows on the dryer, while the rest of the wash dried. Let the warm hum of it take her off somewhere. Followed it wherever it wanted to go.

It wasn't until Gene came home from the service that she had started liking him. He had been just one of the other boys in high school. Tall, dark, bow-legged. Played a little basketball. Got good grades. But really not the kind of guy that too many girls noticed back then. After high school, Maxine worked as a secretary at the American Greetings factory in Danville. Gene came home from the service. A man with four years of serving his country but nobody in Stanford needed his help. So he had turned to factories for work. He met Maxine again when he came into the factory to fill out an application. He came home a different man than Maxine had remembered. A different look in his eye. He was confident and that made him attractive.

What about our time?

Maxine was at the stove mashing up a potato for Mouse. Peeling all the brown skin off, mashing up every bit with a fork. It was a simple task but she concentrated hard, just making sure there was nothing for him to choke on. Before the question, Gene had come through the front door without a greeting. He missed the softness of Maxine's arms around him. He missed her mouth on his before he crossed the threshold.

But what about our time?

Maxine was a blur. He had become accustomed to seeing just the back of her body scooting from room to room. Hands elbow-deep in laundry, her backside bent over the crib, a glimpse of the way her short-cropped hair graced the nape of her long neck. Even at night it was only her back that he saw. Her bare arms and shoulders, the color of baked piecrust. A taste of her neck exposed just above the lace collar of her nightgown. Night after night he reached out to her.

Please Gene not tonight.

Or, at the exact moment that he had finally convinced her to let him just hold her, the baby's cry would intrude.

It was odd, but just when Mouse was finally growing up, just then was when Maxine was about to need Gene again. That's when he had begun to be drawn to the streets, to the bootleg house, to the other women. That's when he had given up trying.

You don't need me Maxine, you got your man right in there.

That night when Mouse was sixteen and Maxine had put Gene out, Eugene pointed his long, dark finger toward Mouse's room. And walked out the door.

This done gone on too long. I ain't cut out for this kind of life. That's our child, Maxine Jean. I love him too. But I'm your husband; I needed a wife.

Maxine pulled another load of clothes out of the dryer.

Spoil their sons and raise their daughters?

She had never had a daughter. She wondered how a girl child would have been different. Would she have loved her any less? The space between Mouse's joyous entrance into this world and this person he had become was an expansive gap. So wide Maxine felt sometimes she would fall over into the space and find herself surrounded by darkness and alone. She saw herself ending up in a hospital. Heartbreak manifesting itself into ulcers or full-blown heart trouble.

Her husband was spending his nights with Honey. He was gone. And Mouse was growing up on her. She had gone from knowing everything to knowing nothing. Her evenings were spent alone. Every time the phone rang it was for Mouse. Girls needing his company. She could hear the pleading in their voices reminding her too much of herself. Junior and Peanut calling him to the hill and wanting to "shoot some hoops." Always something, somebody.

Mouse always comes to dinner waiting for him in the oven. His mother is always waiting on the couch. Seeing him safely in. He retreats to his room and shuts the door, not to be seen until the next morning. All she ever sees is his back and the occasional shrug of his shoulders, or the occasional kiss on the cheek she receives when she questions him. When she pleads for a piece of his time. He will be leaving her house soon, too, following in his father's footsteps.

Maxine is in mourning, grieving for the tiny hands and feet that she used to kiss. She hears little slippered feet pattering down the hallway. Feels little chubby arms wrapped around her knees. Hears the incessant questions.

Mommy, how does the rain stay in the sky before it falls? Is the moon really made out of cheese? Will you play with me?

Sixteen years move in slow motion; then catch speed, fast, like the pages of a book being flipped. At night it is not Gene she misses but the closeness of Mouse. His limp body on her lap, asleep. His head on her breasts. His eyes closed. Long eyelashes. She kisses his sleeping face. Smells baby smells.

She folds his underwear. White, with dark green ovals and octagons. She holds them in the air. Clean. Looks at them and shakes her head. Too big. Much too big.

She hears him before he comes in. Hears his footsteps, slapping against the sidewalk. His long feet slapping, slapping. She has prepared a speech, a good talking to. The back door opens. She feels his hands on her shoulders but she dares not turn around. She feels his kiss on her cheek, thinks there was a hint of stubble. Smells beer on his breath.

"Dinner still in the oven?" he says.

She keeps still, to keep from crumbling. Closes her eyes and takes in his voice. Deep. Scratchy. Some strange voice that she has yet to fully recognize. Some strange man who refuses her, shuns her sweetness.

The Fight

Toni and Candy

The Fight

Before the fight, the house is swarming with Aunt Daphne and her three children. Girl, boy, boy. The girl is three years old and dumpling fat, like me and my sister, Candy. The boys are six and seven, skinny little things, wild as puppies. Aunt Daphne's husband, Leroy, is out in the backyard with my father. Through the side porch window I can see Daddy firing up the grill and Leroy's hands flying up in the air and his lips working ten miles a minute. Daddy's face looks like he's in some physical pain, like he's caught in a wrestler's headlock.

Leroy is not the kind of uncle you call uncle. He's just Leroy. He talks loud and non-stop about everything there ever was like a record player with no 'off' button. The house and the yard are loud, loud, loud and Candy and me are like our father, quiet like birds.

My mother and I are at the kitchen counter, which still has white flour spots from this morning's biscuits. She is mixing the hamburger with chopped onion, spices, a bit of breadcrumbs, and an egg. I am patting out the hamburger meat, forming them into large, round patties and placing them on wax paper, which lines a big green serving platter. Our mother is a culinary magician. She has perfected the art of stretching food. She can feed twelve people with one pound of anything and a few odds and ends. But barbecuing is my father's specialty.

Candy and Aunt Daphne are at the kitchen table. Candy is shucking corn and placing the long blonde silks into a large piece of newspaper and Aunt Daphne is chopping cabbage for coleslaw and has just put the potatoes on the stove to boil.

The kitchen is a mess just like the rest of the house. Mama has never been one for appearances. There is no magic in her cleaning skills. The house is not filthy or nasty. It's just messy. Piles of paper in the corners—bills, articles torn from magazines, mimeographed copies of poems my mother liked in high school, old photographs of Grandpapa before he died, and Mama dressed in pleated, long skirts and sweaters when she was young. Our house is full of things like that, things my mother wants to keep.

There is clean, unfolded laundry on all the beds. All of our dirty clothes are still on the floor in the bathroom from our baths this morning. We are amazed when we visit other people's houses and see things neat and tidy behind closed pantries and shut closets and cabinet doors.

The boy cousins are running through the house playing cowboys and Indians. They are running from the living room to the kitchen over and over in a circle, yeehawing and grinning from cheek to cheek like it's the most fun they've ever had. I hear the coffee table being shifted from its spot. It makes a dragging sound across the hardwood floor in the living room, like fingernails on a blackboard.

My mother and Aunt Daphne keep on talking as if they can't see the hooligans running through the house taking whatever's in their path with them. All this noise wakes the fat baby girl, Isella, who has been asleep on the couch. The toddler who looks so cute in the pictures that Aunt Daphne sends is suddenly transformed into a monster. Her hair is all over her head from her nap and her face has the nubby imprint from the couch fabric. Her face is so torn up that she looks like one of the Sleestacks off Saturday morning TV, her mouth is gaped open to holler. She is red and silent, but when she gasps for breath, a blood-curdling scream comes out. Aunt Daphne grabs her up in her arms like she's a smaller baby than she really is and rocks her over her shoulder.

"Yes, that's Mama's love… Shhh. Brothers waking the baby up." Our cousin is big for her age and looks like a six-year-old with her creased, plump legs sprawled across Aunt Daphne's lap. She goes from screaming to cooing like a dove under Aunt Daphne's open palmed fingers rubbing her back in wide soothing circles.

"Bless her heart," Mama says and smiles that 'I remember when' smile.

Aunt Daphne and my mother are both slender as string beans. It's only when they smile wide smiles and wrinkles form at the edge of their mouths, that you can you tell they are in their forties. They are close, like me and Candy. The only difference is that me and Candy are more heavy-set. Not fat, really, but big boned. At least that's how our mother explains it. "Big boned from your father's side."

Late at night in the glow of the nightlight, in our room, we talk about all the things we could do if we could will ourselves skinny.

"I'd be a model," Candy says. "Walk down the runway with my bony hips. Cameras would flash and I would smile like this." Candy puts on a face that makes her teeth look false and ghostly under the glow of the orange bulb. We sputter and choke with laughter.

"I'd marry the finest thing walking," I say, recovering my breath. "I would live in a big house and I would cook and have babies and all that. I'd be a detective, too, like Christie Love but only I'd have a bigger Afro than hers, wear my Aigner boots and short shorts, have gold earrings big as coffee saucers." I scoop my hands up into the shape of a large circle. "And I'd grin at them, like this." I smiled too, wide enough to make Candy laugh.

We try to keep it low because if we laugh too loudly Daddy

knocks on the wall and threatens to come in and whip us. He never does, no matter what, but we keep it down anyway.

Me and Candy have bunk beds, but when we are in the mood to gab we climb into one bed and whisper out our skinny futures into the dark. I wake up in the middle of the night and kiss Candy on the forehead. She wakes up and kisses me back too. She always thinks I'm asleep but I'm usually playing possum.

We both wish we were like Mama and Aunt Daphne, who don't dress in style any more but would look perfectly good in a mean pair of hip huggers or a body suit. No flab hanging over even with all these kids.

Sometimes me and Candy lie to each other and say, "You look like you lost some inches." We pinkie swear that we'll go on another diet soon but we were never serious about it before the fight.

By the time the sweet pickles are cut into the potato salad and the baked beans are removed from the oven, Daddy is stabbing the blackened meat with a fork and throwing it into a waiting pan; jabbing the steak, the hot dogs, the hamburgers and rubbing his head. Just from looking, from this distance between the back yard and the house, I know that Leroy is not only standing on my daddy's last nerve but jumping up and down on it. Daddy likes it quiet. I lean into Candy and whisper, "Time for a rescue mission," and we carry out the plastic utensils and plates to set the picnic table. Mama and Aunt Daphne are still talking in the living room and the baby is now rounded out in my mother's small lap, spilling over the edges like yeast bread rising.

"Daddy, we got the plates," Candy says as we leave the stuff on the table and head toward the men. Daddy's face is pinched up like he's at his maddest. And Leroy, whose back is slightly turned to us, seems oblivious that he is adding steam to Daddy's pressure cooker.

"... and so I told that fool, man. 'Fool if I ever catch you around my car again' and he shot off straight down the street like a bullet, lickety split. Like a goddam bullet. Like I was telling my friend, Petey, 'Petey, I said, I don't know what I'd do…all these years…'"

"Girls," Daddy turns to us like we're saviors. "Take over for a minute while I go in and use the restroom."

"I got it man."

"These ladies know what they're doing. Don't nobody live in my house and not learn how to cook, especially as much as they eat. Now don't they look like they know how to cook?"

Daddy winks at us.

Leroy laughs like a crazy person and Candy don't say nothing. We are both mad. Well, not really mad, but hurt. Everybody always has some little fat joke to tell. Seems like they all think it's okay. It's not. It still hurts just the same but we play like it doesn't stab us in the heart.

"Daddy, please," I holler back over my shoulder, keeping my smile in place. His belly is round as Buddha's and I say, "look at that" and point.

"I'ma remember that one girl," Daddy says and points his finger toward me. "I'ma get you for that one."

"You girls looking prettier and prettier every time I see you. You hitting them books like you sposed to?" Leroy asks.

"Yeah." We shrug our shoulders.

"You got boyfriends yet?"

"No." Candy looks at me with that *he-is-so-yuck*-look.

Through the backdoor we can see Daddy in the kitchen talking to Mama and this time he's the one with arms flailing in the air. We hear their voices rising but we can't hear exact words. Aunt Daphne is there too, the baby on her hip, playing mediator.

Leroy's tongue is a worm set loose, wiggling it's way through all our business, asking so many questions that Candy and I are lost in his jabber. We try to keep our responses to head nods and three-word answers.

Daddy finally makes his way back, but as Candy and I head for the picnic table, Leroy gets in one last blow.

"Them girls so pretty. Just wait till they lose that baby fat and y'all gonna need a stick to beat off them wild boys."

"I got a shotgun if I need it," Daddy says. But even through his joking we can see that he is angered by something. Something is blowing in the wind.

We have crossed the yard and are about to shut the backdoor before we turn to see our father belly to belly with Leroy, his fist clinched down by his sides.

"Leroy, if you don't shut the hell up, I'm gonna give you something to talk about."

"Come on then, I know you don't want none of me."

"Mama, Leroy and Daddy are about to fight," Candy yells. "Right in the yard," I add, knowing the words make no sense even as they are coming out.

"Lord, God—come on Daphne! They are so crazy."

"Stupid ass men all these years and they still can't get along for ten minutes."

Mama and Aunt Daphne are into the yard before we know it. Aunt Daphne has passed Isella to me. I am holding her with my hip jutted out, trying to balance the weight. Candy is talking to her and grabbing her chubby fingers into her hand.

"It's okay, Baby Isella," she coos, "your Mama'll be back in a minute."

Isella's lips are puckering slightly, one of her arms reaching for her mother.

I shift my weight again and bounce. She's really a cute baby.

"Hi girly girl," I say. She seems to like the sound. "Hi girly, girly, girly." If that's what keeps her from crying, I'll do it until Aunt Daphne comes to get her.

"What in the hell is going on?" Aunt Daphne steps between Daddy and Leroy facing Leroy. Mama is in charge of Daddy.

"Y'all are too old to be acting this way."

"Don't he ever shut his damned mouth?"

"Man, I ain't done nothing to you. You better keep your hands to your self. Daphne, you better tell this fool something."

"I'm going to tell you both something. The children are watching."

All the grown ups turn toward us. I am balancing Isella like a large box, wedging her on my hip. Candy is standing with her arms folded, waiting to see what happens next. The boys are in the house doing God only knows what.

But it is over before it gets started. Daddy is back tending the food and Leroy is walking around in the yard a few feet from him, cooling off.

At dinner, Leroy is back at full speed talking about nothing to nobody in particular and everybody at the same time.

"This potato salad is good. Y'all ever had that potato salad in the store. Now that is some awful mess, tastes like paste. No flavor. No salt. No mustard. We had this picnic at work and I was telling this guy I work with, 'Man this tastes like glue.' It did too. Just like some paste or something. Awful." Leroy screws up his face just like Baby Isella had earlier.

Me and Candy are sitting by each other and just for that purpose, as a Leroy shield. We roll our eyes at each other. We communicate with our eyes and decide not to talk unless we have to.

Mama has Aunt Daphne. They are carrying on their own conversation about how long they were in labor, even while Leroy is talking.

"Lord, girl, I thought Candy was never gonna make it out. I was in labor for 48 hours. I know you remember that. Probably got the scars still on your wrists to prove it." Mama laughs a cackly young laugh.

Daddy is putting all his energy into an ear of corn, concentrating on blocking out both conversations. At least that is what I think he's doing.

"And ain't nothing worse than bad potato salad or bad mashed potatoes. Now you would think folks couldn't mess up mashed potatoes but they can."

"And look at her now," Aunt Daphne says. "Look at both of them now. Wouldn't ever believe either of them started out this big." Aunt Daphne snaps her fingers. "No bigger than a minute." She looks at me and Candy like we're Mama's prizes. And Mama smiles at us like we are. Like she always does when she remembers us in plaits and baby walking shoes.

The boys have each other; fat Isella is bounced on Aunt Daphne's knee and has a long string of slobber slivering toward the table. Daddy is sulled up like a bullfrog.

"Good, God, Daphne do y'all have to talk about childbirth at the eatin table?" Leroy shakes his head. Aunt Daphne glares at him but acts like he hasn't spoken a word.

"She," Aunt Daphne nods toward Isella, "was my hardest. All back labor all up in here." She rubs the small of her back and makes a face like she's feeling the pain again.

"All that time," Mama says, "and you had only dilated four centimeters."

"Uh huh, exactly."

Mama and Aunt Daphne go back and forth like this and ooh and ahh like they are in a room full of women telling these birthing stories for the first time.

The boys are playing with their food.

"Mama, I don't like this; it tastes like it's got dirt clods in it. See?" one of them says and spits the potato salad into his hand.

"Shit, Miles." Aunt Daphne tries to catch him before he rubs it into the picnic table and mixes it with the baby's slobber.

"Daphne, baby, get that boy. Damn it, boy. Now why is he doing that, Daphne? Daphne get the boy! My God. I'll be damned. Ain't got a bit of table manners. I'll be damned."

"Leroy, please."

Daddy sucks air through his teeth and takes his frustration out on his hamburger. He bites it hard and shakes his head. Mama eyes Daddy but don't say nothing to him.

"I'll be damned, boy."

"Daddy, it tastes like dirt."

"Boy, you don't know good food when you see it. When I was a little boy like you I ate what was put before me. Didn't say a word."

Aunt Daphne shakes her head, scowls, and keeps up her conversation with Mama.

Leroy's diatribe is much more embarrassing than anything that little Miles has done.

Miles tucks his chin close to his chest.

Aunt Daphne is one of those mothers with octopus arms, she is cleaning up Miles' mess and doing all this while holding the giant baby and shushing the other boy, Marquez, before he does the same thing, all-the-while keeping a conversation going with Mama and occasionally glaring at Leroy.

"Good Lord," my mother says, in a teenager's voice that we rarely witness. She and Aunt Daphne cup their hands around their mouths and giggle. They are wearing the same shade of brick-colored lipstick like thirteen-year-old girlfriends. My mother and Aunt Daphne whisper in each other's ears. They block the rest of us out and talk about people and things that only they can understand.

Mama becomes playful when Aunt Daphne is around. Aunt Daphne and Leroy come to visit from Cincinnati once or twice a year. It has always seemed to be a chore for my father. I look at these women and wonder what they were like when they were little. I can't see ever being away from Candy.

That night Candy and me settle into our beds and the day becomes a collection of memories to be stored away. The bad boys. Isella, the screaming baby girl. Leroy. The smell of my mother's baked beans and my father's secret sauce. Mama looking as though she was about to cry when she waved bye-bye to Aunt Daphne from the driveway. Daddy's discontent. With the memories stored away, all the world is right again. I feel the warmth of Candy's familiar body next to mine. We are bedtime-clean and donned in our favorite pink pajamas whispering quietly, not knowing that our lives are about to change. I cling to the memory of this moment even now because it is the last time I remember feeling totally certain about my place in the world.

In the moments that followed, our parents' voices grew from the familiar inaudible mumbles to full-fledged war words that left us all scarred.

"How am I sposed to feel?" My father's voice quivers with rage. "How in the fuck am I supposed to feel?"

"I don't know how you are supposed to feel," My mother screams, "What's done is done. It's a long time ago. What can I do about it now?"

"Every time the son-of-a-bitch comes down here. He throws it in my face. Did you have to tell your sister everything? You told her and she told him. I don't want to hear his mouth every single goddamn time."

"Bennie, what do you want me to do about it?"

"Janice, I don't know. All I know is that they are both my girls. They're my babies no matter what." We had never heard our father cry before.

"Bennie, they are always going to be your girls, both of them. You're her father too."

My sister and I grow cold underneath the covers and hug each other. We all cry together. One of us is not our father's real child. We feel our parents' hearts breaking through the wall that separates us.

The next morning, a Sunday, Mama cooks breakfast. A mound of bacon, scrambled eggs, toast, buttered on both sides, bacon gravy and fried apples. Our mother cooks over the half-filled baked beans dish, the rank bowl of potato salad; all the barbeque utensils from yesterday like they are not there at all. She is our regular mom, pleasant, but yesterday's giddiness has drained. All the tears too. She's living life in neutral again. My father seems normal too. Nothing is spoken about last night's revelation and me and my sister watch our father place his arms around our mother's small waist and plant kisses on her neck. Candy and I are afraid to ask, hoping it's a dream that will float away. In the whiteness of daylight, last night seems surreal. I look at Candy and shrug my shoulders when nobody's looking. She is glassy-eyed and bewildered but we all hold up this farce through breakfast and seemingly, so far, for the rest of our lives.

By late summer, Candy and I grow tired of searching through our mother's old pictures and putting our ears up to the walls trying to seek more information. We even eavesdrop on the other line when Mama talks to Aunt Daphne. Still we know no more than we learned that night.

The second Saturday in August is back to school time. Me, Candy and my mother have sat on the porch all day long watching the other families and their kids carrying in bags loaded down with blue jeans, skirts, blouses and shirts, number two pencils, and reams and reams of notebook paper in bright pink, blue and green. It is one of the hottest days of the year and we are on the porch swing and our mother is rocking gently back and forth trying to make a breeze in this sweltering heat. We are each sipping a glass of fresh lemonade and waving at the neighbors as they arrive and depart from their houses. We watch the boys climb into cars with their parents, with mad on their faces. Boys hate this time of year. We watch the girls and their mothers drive off together. We even see someone we don't know pick up Jeanette Stokes.

But this is a time of rest for us. Our dresses are already pressed and hanging ready for church. The house is clean, as clean as it gets around here, and Daddy is napping in a lawn chair in the backyard. The yard is mowed and we are all waiting for five o'clock when Daddy will fire up the grill and we'll bring the boiled meat from the kitchen, the hot dogs and the perfectly round beef patties that are waiting in the refrigerator. School is about to start and we are prepared. Our mother finished our shopping in June. Candy and I are two sizes smaller. When we tried on our new bras last night we both marveled at each other's smooth lines—not hardly any flab at all, only a tad bit on both of us around the middle.

While our parents dig into the heavy meal and make small talk about the weather, a neighborhood softball game and church, Candy and I nibble at our meat and fill our plates with salad. Neither of our parents notice who we've become. Tonight we'll sleep with the lamp on. It is our new normal. Our whispered conversations are inventions of what our mother's lover looks like. Tall, short, young, old. Brown-skinned, light-skinned. We invent worlds where our mother engages with her man, the man that is one of our fathers.

"Maybe he is a poet from up in New York, who was a speaker at the library and she couldn't resist his love poems," Candy whispers.

"No, why would he be here in Kentucky at Stanford's library? No, he was her high school sweetheart, you know, the one that daddy use to tease her about."

A traveling preacher who gave a guest sermon at the church. Somebody Mama works with down at the creamery. The plumber from over in Crab Orchard who's tall and light and looks like a movie star. The truck driver who broke down at the bottom of the hill one time. We do this every night.

Sometimes we stare at each other without blinking to try and figure it out, trying to find the father in one of our faces. While she is sleeping, I look at Candy and wonder which of us is the real daughter. A flash of jealousy rises in me when I think I spot Daddy in her face but then I kiss her just the same. When I try to fall asleep, I can't. I lay awake and watch Candy sleeping like she's at peace, like she holds the real answer inside her like a secret. I want to shake her to wake her up and ask but I don't dare. Candy and me have always been the same, almost like twins, yet I can't help but think that somewhere inside our bodies, inside our hearts; something is growing and stretching out of shape between us like a rubber band, stressed and pulled so tight that there is nothing left to do but snap.

Sixteen Confessions of Lois Carter

Lois

Sixteen Confessions of Lois Carter

I

My mother never approved but she came to like Roscoe, even after trying hard not to. When Roscoe had his gallbladder surgery, Mother came over and helped me out around the house. In the kitchen, with just the two of us washing up the supper dishes, Mother patted my hand and told me that Roscoe was a good person. "He's gonna be fine," she said to me, "don't you worry." And she looked in on Roscoe before she left. She stood in the middle of the floor, near the bed but not too close, and stared at him. I have never known if she was wishing Daddy alive at that moment or if she was having some silent "make up" session with Roscoe. He was snoring lightly underneath the covers, sleeping off the anesthesia. She whispered, "I love you," to me like a secret, gathered her gloves and purse and went.

2

My brother hasn't spoken to me in years, not since Roscoe. And I've given up trying. Jimmy lives in Knifley with his wife and kids. I both miss him and hope never to lay eyes on him again. I hear about him through my sisters. They like the wife but Jimmy ain't changed a bit. This marriage is one issue he can't be budged on. I look at old pictures sometimes and remember us playing tag out in the back yard. His hair straight as a poker, long as a girl's. As a big sister, it was my duty to hold him down and make him let me comb and brush his hair. He was my baby doll. We played hide-and-go-seek. He loved me then. When all us kids worked down at the store, it was me whose skirt tails he clung to. I wore an apron when I worked the cold cuts. I've made many a bologna or hog's head cheese sandwich with Jimmy moving in and out of the front flap of my apron, his jaws beet-red. He would run up and give me kisses when I bent down to stock the low shelves. Jimmy used to call me Lewis instead of Lois when he was little. He don't call me nothing now. Nothing I'd want to hear.

3

Roscoe and I met in 1969. We were both seniors. Integration was cutting its baby teeth. Mostly we stayed to ourselves within groups of our own color unless it was something that involved the girls just being with black girls or the boys being together. There was no mixing of the sexes except to speak nervously in the hallway. We didn't know much about the colored kids and they didn't know much about us. They both intrigued and frightened me. I had never gone to school with black kids before.

Roscoe was in my science class. Mrs. Kiesler was our teacher. Old as dirt. Pink cat-eyed glasses. A thin, haggardly look. Her hair was long and gray. She kept it up in a mound of extended beehive looking like one of those holy-roller women from up off the ridge where my mother grew up. Big, high hair and two sprigs of curlicues at each cheek, right in front of her ears. It was her goal to stump all of us, especially the blacks but Roscoe always had the right answer. He already knew all there was to know about photosynthesis and mollusk traits and invertebrates and zygote division. And he knew how to use the microscope without squeezing one eye shut or going cross-eyed. "Very good, Roscoe," Mrs. Kiesler said aloud one day more enthusiastically than she meant to when Roscoe was the only person in the class who could name the three types of amphibians. She couldn't help herself. Science was her passion and Roscoe's attention to her lessons overwhelmed her. I was proud. I tried to keep my joy to myself but I couldn't. I loved him even then.

4

My sister, Thelma, and me talk pretty near every week. She's a hairdresser over in Danville. She can't have children, so she doted on mine and now has moved on to the grandkids. My other sister? Well Irene and me are cordial. I see her on Christmas, Easter and Thanksgiving. We call to check in and make sure nobody's sick or nobody's dead or dying. We see each other mostly at funerals, reunions and during the holidays but she never let their kids spend the night. Not even once. Something we've never talked about, not even once, but I think about it all the time. Sometimes when I'm in Thelma's chair getting my hair washed and set and she's talking up a storm, I wish Irene was there too. Three sisters cutting up. What's more sisterly than getting your hair done but it never happens.

5

My parents worked hard building up their store. Had me stocking cans of cling peaches and green beans before I could even read the labels. It was the kind of store where you can get hamburger and eggs on credit. All the little black kids use to come in and get pop, potato chips, nabs and nickel candy after school and I couldn't hardly work for staring at them, trying to figure out how their hair stayed that way or how long it took their mothers to put all those little rainbow plastic barrettes in their hair. They were different, yeah, but not in the ways my parents thought. In those days I wanted to be on their side of the counter, just to see what it was like. Now I know. Well no, I guess I'll never know, exactly, but I do know what it feels like to be different.

My father eyed them like he thought they were going to steal something but all the snacks and the things that children loved were right there in front of the counter. In the aisles where my father lurked, peering over at the children, were the grown up produce: Quaker oats, Wonder bread, Carnation milk, Ivory soap, little boxes of Tide detergent, Close-up toothpaste, a few ladies products (as my mother called them) and rows and rows of canned fruits and vegetables. The children would buy their candy and stand around and talk. My father would shoo them out of the store. "Y'all go on home, now." Then mumble, "Damn little darkies," under his breath. Mother wouldn't be so obvious but after they were gone she would pull out her cleaning rag and wipe down everything she had seen them touch.

6

My father died when I was fourteen. My mother always said he was turning over in his grave. At night when I pray, I ask God to help make my father understand and let him know I'm all right. I love my daddy still. In a perfect world, I see us sitting at the supper table eating pot roast and cornbread as the sun sets on a Sunday evening. Afterwards, me and Mother tending the kids, Roscoe and Daddy out on the porch talking about sports or cars or a basketball game. But that is in my dream world. In my real world even if my father was alive I don't think those things would happen. Not on this planet anyway.

7

Five or six kids came in the store one time and in the shuffle, they left one of the little ones behind. He was crying but was able to tell us his name and where he lived. My mother insisted I walk him home. It was right at springtime, those days when it's cold in the mornings and warm enough in the afternoon to get rid of your sweater. His name was Syrus. I said his name over and over not really to comfort him but to hear its strange sound roll off my own tongue. His name wasn't Bill or Johnny or Luke. Syrus. Syrus took my hand when we were outside the store and walking across the backfield. He seemed scared. His hand was warm, warmer than my little brother's and moist. I looked at our hands together, his just a few shades darker than mine and I remember noticing but thinking both our hands were just *hands*. Who cared about skin?

8

My mother-in-law cleans up for us every weekend but I don't need her to cook. I can cook as good as any woman. But she cooks anyway and I let her. But I hate it. Every Sunday after church, after we've changed out of our church clothes, she rearranges my kitchen to suit her needs and she lies on my couch while the turkey is cooking or the chicken is frying, the oil in her press-and-curl easing into my couch. Her sweet tea is too sweet. She tastes all the food and puts the spoon back. She is killing Roscoe with all that pork. She still puts it in everything. What I hate more than all of this is that I feel as if I can't say a word. It won't go over well.

9

Miss Pearline, she looks at me sometimes and I can see it in her eyes that she's saying: *You took my son from me*! She's always been accepting, even when all this started and I stayed with her and Mr. Givens when my own mother said, "It just ain't right. I can't have no daughter of mine seeing no niggra. What would your Daddy say, Lois?"

Been a blue million years now and that still gives me the shakes just thinking about it. But on days when I'm in the kitchen with Miss Pearline and it's clear that I've been brought up to make gravy one way and she's been brought up to make it another, I can see it in her eyes that she wishes her son had married a black woman.

10

Even now, when I'm up in age, people from all over come up to me when I'm out and say, "Ain't you one of them Carter girls?"

At the onset their smiles are wide, remembering my folks and Carter's Grocery but just as soon as they recognize me as the one who did *that*, their smiles drop. They clear the mucus from their throats and move on about their business. I don't say a word. Too tired to fight back these days. But I hope to God they don't think I don't notice it at all.

11

I caught Miss Pearline once. I saw her once hugging the neck of one of Roscoe's old girlfriends, one of the black ones. She hugged her neck tight like she wanted her to be her son's wife so bad. When she pulled away, I caught her crying. She cried a grieving cry. We were at a church over in Lexington. I was just about the only white woman there. I looked out across the congregation and caught another white woman's eye but I never said hello to her. I somehow felt like everybody would know why I did. Not that it would matter but I didn't want to call more attention to myself. After the benediction,

Roscoe went to the restroom and I made the long walk through the crowd toward our car. I saw Miss Pearline hugging that woman, like she was something precious lost. Maybe it was all for some other reason. Something I don't know. Maybe I'm being paranoid but I'm sure I'm right. If it wasn't like I saw it, I wish somebody could prove me wrong.

12

Me and Roscoe were an accident waiting to happen. He was my lab partner and I was the dumb one. He covered my butt every time. One time we were down in the library like all the other kids in our class, working side by side, and I walked over to read the directions over his shoulder. It wasn't cologne exactly but Roscoe smelled sweet and I could feel the heat as he unexpectedly turned around at the same time I leaned. Our heads nearly butted, but inside, my mind was made up before I even knew what I was thinking about.

I had kissed other boys but nothing more. A bunch of us had gotten together to study over at Susan Beard's house. Her parents hadn't even balked at Roscoe being among us. The basement was where Susan's bedroom was. Their basement was paneled and there was a sitting room at the bottom of the steps: couch, chair, coffee table, and a large dinette table with chairs that we gathered around to study. The Beard parents left the house to pick up groceries. The other kids left. Susan Beard went to take a shower for her date. Roscoe was about to leave. But we brushed together again before he left and we ended up on Susan Beard's couch. After the kiss, everything else was quick—clothes not off but shifted, no music, no romance; no 'I love you's' whispered into each other's ears. We spent the next three days pretending it never happened at all.

On our wedding night Roscoe confessed that it had been his first time, too, and how he had left so quickly because he thought something had happened to him when he climaxed. What about me? I laughed but never told him that I thought I was going to bleed to death. That first night I had prayed to God that by morning my parents wouldn't find me dead in my bed.

13

Me and Roscoe still have sex every Thursday morning. Early. Even before the sun peeks up and turns red. If I were to be honest with myself, I am still startled by Roscoe when I wake up next to him. I always keep the bathroom light on so I can clearly see his dark skin glistening in the sheer light of morning against my own. I touch the short, tight curls against his scalp. Look into his eyes, warm black pools. All this surprises me even after thirty some odd years. Roscoe and me. We've come through too much to talk about any of that out loud, but a woman can have a private thought if she wants to.

14

Our grandchildren, we have three now, are blessed because they are a mixture. I can look at them and see Roscoe clear as day but I can see myself too, my mother even. The eldest has my mother's green eyes and my red hair. I am glad. Not because she's light-skinned but because I overhear them talk about being black. They don't ever talk about being white. Glad some of them can't deny their other side. Can't deny me. Makes me happy. Happier than it should.

15

I am a chameleon. I move in and out of all my selves. With Thelma at the beauty shop I'm a white woman, just a plain white woman. In there we are all the same. We laugh and cut up and have fun but when I'm at Shirley's or Frieda's, I'm somebody different all together. When we sip our iced tea and lemonade and play Tonk and talk about our men, I think they forget that I'm white. I like those times; that's when I'm at my happiest, laughing and having fun with my girls. Both sets of them. I live one life over there, one over here. I live my life straddled. Never standing too straight or tall in either world. The two hardly ever mix. I love my girls, though, both sets. Roscoe hates to come home to a hen party or to come home to find me gone to one, but he knows I know where home is.

16

When Mother died, people came from all over, bringing baskets of food and flowers, looking at Roscoe and me like we were the reason she was dead. My brother got drunk at the wake and called Roscoe out of his name, something the others didn't have enough liquor in them to do. Roscoe and me left. The whole place smelled of dying roses and made me sick to my stomach. I dream about that. Only in my dream Mother is alive, and she steps out from behind my brother and puts her finger to her lips for me to be quiet. Even in death, she is the peacemaker. Or maybe she is urging me not to talk about it. And I don't talk about it anymore. No use. I dream that over and over, but I'm not sure why. If Mother knew me at all, she would know that I have spent what seems like a lifetime holding my tongue.

Respite

Pearline

Respite

It is July. At the onset, Pearline Givens looked upon her respite as a death sentence. The problem began with a nosebleed while watching the lunchtime news with Hazel, her next-door neighbor and best friend. Pearline had thought nothing of it at first, and then the headache came, followed by a dizzy spell.

Hazel called the life squad to take Pearline to the hospital. The doctors said it was her high blood pressure. So there she was, caught between the devil and a rock. The doctors advised that she shouldn't be alone while she recovered. Thus her predicament: an extended stay with Roscoe and Lois.

It was nearly one hundred degrees outside and Pearline was resting on the couch under the air conditioning. The couch, a beige thing sprouting large orange and aqua flowers, is soft and deep like a pillow. Pearline's long, arthritic legs were stretched beyond the limits of the arms, the back of her hand draped over her forehead, trying to quell the headache. But it was a guarded rest. This was not her couch, her living room. It belonged to her son and his wife. The couch was in fact better than anything she had at home but not nearly as comfortable. She longed for her little, one bedroom, A-frame house in Lancaster where she could find her things and have them handy.

Roscoe carries her bags through the door of the spare bedroom, where they have prepared for Pearline's stay, clean sheets and pillowcases, her own emerald green towels folded neatly on the bed. When she enters the room, Pearline feels like crying. It's one of the kids' old rooms with the Tweety and Bugs Bunny, the teenage heartthrob posters, young men showing hairless chests, still on the wall.

"There you go, Mama," Roscoe says placing her plaid suitcase on the bed, standing with his legs gaped and his arms folded over his chest, like his daddy for the world, "You're all settled."

"Thank you, baby," Pearline manages but she was far from settled. Her insides are churning like clabbered milk and she has left her antacids at home, she only takes one kind, the white ones that come in the square bottle. Lord only knows what kind of stuff they have in their medicine cabinet. No telling. "Lord, God," she says to herself in a whisper so low that even she could barely hear it.

"You say something, Mama?"

"Naw." Pearline sighed and sat on the edge of the bed and looked up at the child's florescent stars and moons on the ceiling. "I swear 'fore God…" she mumbled.

"Mama, are you talking to yourself?"

"I'm old enough to talk to myself, to listen, and to answer myself back if that's what I want to do."

Roscoe smiled at his mother's sass. Lois peeked her head in the door and looped her arm through Roscoe's like they were about to walk down the aisle again. She placed her head on his shoulder, a ringlet of red curls falling on his chest. Pearline thinks they are too old to be acting like this, full-grown children and grandchildren taboot. She looks away from them, embarrassed, and feels the blood rising up in her face.

"All settled, Miss Pearline?"

"Settled. Yes, I'm settled. I'm sure you young folks have better things to do than fool with an old woman like me. Don't y'all mind me. Go on and do what you usually do." Pearline turned her back to them and began unpacking her clothes. She turns her body a bit more, so that Roscoe can't see that she's unpacking her underwear and placing them in the top drawer of the blue and yellow child's bureau.

When Roscoe and Lois leave the room, Pearline closes the door behind them and leans back on it for support. Even with the door closed, she hears them 'babying and sugaring' like love-sick kids; the God-awful sound of the television changing (young people don't know how to sit and watch one station); and later, Lois rattling pots and pans like it was the first time she had ever cooked in her life. Pearline peeped out and yelled toward the hallway that led to the kitchen. "Lois, baby, you need some help cookin?"

"Rest Miss Pearline, I been cookin all my life. Don't you worry yourself—you just rest."

And Roscoe is sitting on his behind in their brown leather recliner chair watching TV like it was a vault full of money, changing the stations just as fast as he can go.

Pearline doesn't come out until supper and what a supper it is. No salt on the chicken. No meat in the green beans. No bread, not a crumb. No sugar in the tea. Pearline takes a bite of her chicken and tries to chew, tries to swallow but finally excuses herself and blames the headache.

The next morning, after Roscoe and Lois leave for work, Pearline emerges from the room to explore the house. Everything here is familiar, Pearline's been in this house many times over the years, yet staying here, no matter for how short a period of time, is a whole different story. This house is too big. With the kids gone, Roscoe and Lois should move to a smaller place like she did when Pete died. All these gadgets. Light switches that move up and down and go from midnight to sunrise. Who ever heard of such?

In the bathroom, Pearline finds five different kind of hair things that plug in on Lois's side of the storage cabinet: blow dryer, crimping iron and three different kinds of curling irons. Roscoe has just as many electrical things on his side: hair clippers, shavers, electric teeth cleaners. Pearline balances herself and steps over into the shower, where she stands for ten minutes trying to figure out which knob simply turns the water on, which was all she needed.

After her shower, Pearline peeps in the medicine cabinets, marvels at the fluff of the towels, and sniffs Lois's perfumed concoctions—a variety of bubble baths and bath salts, shampoos and splashes that rest alongside the tub. She shakes her head in half disgust, half amazement and continues to meddle.

In the bedroom, she scoffs at the thread count of the sheets and dresses. She puts on one of the dresses she brought with her—one she wears to church. She didn't feel like putting on one of her housedresses and walking around in this fancy place.

In the kitchen she finds that Lois has cooked breakfast for her. *Sweet child, bless her heart,* Pearline thinks until she sees the poached egg rising above the fancy plate like a clouded sunrise, the tiny sparkling glass of orange juice and the toast, dry as a bone, no butter, no jelly. Underneath the plate is a folded note: *For your jumpstart, Miss Pearline. Healthy eating, Love Lois.* Pearline tries, but figures that it would be better to not eat at all than to try to make her way through this tasteless breakfast. She reaches into the cabinet for a larger glass so she can at least have a proper serving of orange juice and the first large plastic tumbler she grabs slides through her hand. "Lord, God," she says and notices the spots on the plates. Immediately there is a mission to be completed. Pearline runs the water and rewashes every dish in Lois's cabinet.

Stepping out into the sun, Pearline adjusts her scarf around her chin; she looks up at the sky and breathes in the morning. This is the first of her daily walks. She must hurry before the sun gets too high in the sky and it gets hot. She makes her way down Water Street, nodding at the neighbors. Some wave, some speak, but they are all curious about her. She is tall and thin, slightly humped; a bent tree stalk in the wind. Her pleated Sunday dress billows out around her in the breeze and she steadies the scarf with one hand and the dress with the other and balances her arm purse in the bend of her elbow.

"Miss Givens, is that you, Roscoe's mama?" Sandy Crawford yells out to her while digging around in her flowerbed.

"Last time I checked it was me, sure enough," Pearline says with her step high, her gait steady. She doesn't have a free hand so she nods hello to Sandy Crawford and keeps on walking.

"You need a ride somewhere, Miss Givens?" Sandy Crawford smiles at her the way old people smile at dancing babies.

"Nope, just out strolling, getting my exercise."

"Well you have a nice day Miss Givens. You be careful."

The people on Water Street that are out in their yards and driveways, follow Pearline until she's all the way down the street and turning the corner.

The sky is a perfect ocean blue. Pearline turns off Water Street, crosses the railroad tracks onto Maxwell and follows Maxwell to Lancaster Street. Her walk is a thinking walk. Steady and determined. With each step Pearline considers her life and how long it has taken her to get to this point. The beginnings of helplessness, she thinks. Roscoe and Lois are already grabbing her at the elbows every time she moves. In her mind she sees the struggle laid out before her. She has watched too many of her friends wither and become second children to their offspring. Lifeless and unresponsive. Being whisked around like grandchildren. With them everything must be done quickly. Anything slow is deemed old and worthless.

Every few yards Pearline stops, places her hands on her hips and gets her breath. This is a journey she's on. One she must complete. She takes her time, stops to gander at the flowerbeds in the front yards along the way. When she reaches Carter's Grocery Pearline enters, grabs a basket and begins shopping. In the cart she places jowl bacon, a tiny shaker of salt, a package of antacids, and a pound of butter. She nods at the young man at the counter, double checks her change and makes her way back to Roscoe's house. When she returns, she eases down the basement steps and stores her goods in the back of the old refrigerator where Roscoe keeps fish bait and beer.

By September, Pearline grows less and less impatient with her family. Although she still doesn't like their ways. Lois puts her clothes in that dryer when she has a perfectly hung clothesline in the backyard. She leaves strands of her long red hair in the sink and she makes white gravy instead of brown when she makes gravy at all. And the food, poor child, no wonder Roscoe is so skinny. The woman should be foundered on salads by now. So Pearline sneaks in and makes smothered pork chops and slips a ham bone into Lois's greens. Pearline knows it angers Lois, but as an old woman and Roscoe's mother, Pearline believes she has that privilege.

"Miss Pearline, let me help you to your room," Lois says when Pearline's in the way in the kitchen and she tries to grab Pearline by the elbow and lead her back to the bedroom.

"I'm fine. I'm alright."

"You need your rest, come over here to the couch then and put your feet up. Watch the *Price Is Right* or one of your other shows." All this comes delivered with the biggest, fakest teeth-gnashing grin that Pearline has ever seen. A "this is about all I can bear," smile. Lois gives Roscoe one of her "do something" looks and here his ass comes running.

"Mama, why don't you sit here on the couch and I'll get you a bowl and you can cut and peel the potatoes. That'll be a help. Won't it Lois?"

Pearline knows if Lois had her druthers she'd not want her to help at all. But she says, "Sure," and Pearline is relegated to potato-peeling duty.

Roscoe is not any better, following behind that woman like he was a duckling falling in behind the mama duck. And watching that television like his life depends on it, not staying on one station for five minutes.

And the kids and the grandkids, sweet as they are, running in and out like wild cats. No home training whatsoever. Grandma can I have a dollar? Mama will you watch the kids? Daddy can I borrow two hundred dollars? *Borrow, my Lord.*

Later after supper, after Roscoe and Lois have gone to bed, Pearline sneaks in and rewashes the dishes. She refuses to eat out of plates half washed, no matter how fancy they are. It is all she can do to sit in the living room and watch *Lawrence Welk* reruns. So after the lights are out. After all that *Mama, Granny, Miss Pearline, Ain't you sleepy*? After the banging noises that Lois and Roscoe make up in the night, Pearline creeps into the kitchen and quietly fills the sink up with hot water like dishes are supposed to be washed in and feels in the cabinet, searching for the ones that the daughter-in-law has half washed. When she lands on a greasy glass or a bowl with remnants of food stains on its underside she smiles a victory smile and slips the dirty dish into the sudsy water.

Pearline never liked housework when she was a young mother and wife but now washing the dishes helps her think, calms her insides somehow. After she's done drying, she puts the still-hot-to-the-touch dishes away in the cabinet, careful to follow Lois's storing patterns even if she doesn't agree. Bowls with the cups? Whoever heard of such? Any woman worth a damn knows that you put the cups with the glasses. You drink out of both of them don't you? Pearline shakes her head, but this isn't her house. She's just a visitor on respite.

After she's done, she hides the dishtowel in the bottom of the dirty clothes and lies out on the couch in the dark for a few minutes before she heads to her bedroom at the far end of the house. It's too hot in there for Pearline and the bed's too little and too hard. And every time she raises the window up, somebody comes up with a solution. *Miss Pearline-Mama-Granny*, they say, *you are going to catch the pneumonia.* So she's learned to lift it just enough so the bottom of the windowsill and the window don't quite meet. It let's a breeze through and the young intruders don't know the difference. Seems chilly in here, they say, but they don't know why. Pearline sits on the bed or in the chair looking straight out into the air like she doesn't hear one blessed word.

At night she lies on the bed and counts every single one of them stars on the ceiling. In the dark they glow up there like real stars. Depending on her eyesight, sometimes they are just white blurry spots but she knows they are there. It is lonely in the dark but that is the time when Pearline gathers her strength. She likes to sleep in the dark, dark. That is when she remembers all her friends who have died; that is when she can reach out and touch Pete's ears again even if it's only in her dreams. She knows that being asleep is as close to death as the living get so she lies there still, testing it out. Sometimes she can't help but to picture Roscoe and Lois's faces if they should find her come morning dead to this world. But all her thoughts are not this murky. This is also the time when she remembers dancing the jitterbug with Pete up in Lexington on their twenty-fifth anniversary. How proud she was when Roscoe won the science fair. Sometimes she remembers her childhood and when she had girl-wonder about the length of the stars away from the earth, why flower blooms look like little faces, how a whole world could be inside of one dew drop.

At 11 A.M. the phone rings, of course it's Hazel.

"When you coming home? This week?"

"Don't rightly know Hazel, working on my blood pressure. Doctor says it ain't come down much but it's improving." Pearline was leery at first but now she's pleased with this new fangled contraption of a phone. She can wash dishes and clean up after her self and talk on the phone all at the same time. Hazel don't like it so much. She can tell when Pearline is only half talking to her and doing something else.

"Loreen's got that cough again. They put her in the hospital. Guess her kids will be over here fetchin her too before long. That'll leave just me and old man Belcher down this way. Least till you get back. You are coming back, ain't you? I can't believe Loreen. I told her to turn up that heat. A little bit of light bill ain't going to kill her. You know she's got tons of money stashed?"

"Uh huh." Pearline is convinced of it, but still doesn't want to gossip about Loreen.

"You coming back ain't you Pearline?"

"Don't know when, Hazel."

"Did you know that Mr. Jackson died? They found him in his bathroom. They said he was reaching for his heart pills, bless his heart."

"We all gonna die, Hazel," Pearline pauses because the truth shouldn't always be told. "One of these days."

"Ain't that the truth."

The women sit in silence for a while and Pearline settles herself in the chair in front of the television. It's almost noon. Time to watch the news. Back in Harrodsburg they always did it in person with Ritz crackers and pimento cheese and glasses of sweet iced tea. They sat on Pearline's tweed couch and traded rheumatism remedies and body ailments between commercials. Now this is how they do it:

"You got it on, Hazel?"

"Hold on. Let me change the station."

Pearline reclines the chair and sits her glass of Diet Coca-Cola up on the TV tray. She likes the feel of the leather underneath her hands. She flips the TV on with the remote control. It's taken her awhile but she's got it now. She can work that thing as good as the rest of them although she can't see them little numbers but the arrows are big and she pushes until she gets her station. She can hear Hazel's, "Oh Lordy," as she rises from her chair and makes it across the room to change the television.

"My knee is killing me," she starts and then says, "Lord and Jesus look at that fire," before the news anchor begins the full story. He's the anchor that Hazel and Pearline like. The one Pearline had tried to tell Roscoe about, but he had just patted her on the hand like you would a lost puppy's head.

"Uh huh, Mama," he says when he ain't heard a damn thing she's said—a disrespectful child at times.

"That fire reminds me of when I was a little girl and we lived out Boneyville and I was living with Mama and Daddy and all us little children were scared to death standing with our mama and daddy watching our house burn clean to the ground. I was the saddest little girl in the world. My doll burnt up in that fire. The only doll I ever did have."

"Well, Hazel that's been a long time ago."

"Fire is something you don't ever get over. Some things you don't ever get over. You know what I mean, Pearline?"

"I sure do, Hazel. Yes I do."

Pearline keeps up with her own little memories that get triggered by the news but she don't speak all out loud like Hazel does.

A picture of the Governor reminds her of the time her mother rode a horse from Harrodsburg to Frankfort to work at the Governor's mansion, helping cook for some big shindig they were putting on. Her mother had returned with stories for days about what the house looked like.

And the robbery reminded her of that time Esther Jenkins got robbed, and cornered the thieves with a skillet till the law came.

And the forecast of rain brought back to her the flood and the great snow of 1976 or was it 1975? Anyhow she remembered being stuck in the house for thirty-some odd days. Her and Pete. That was before Pete died, before she moved back to Harrodsburg where she was born and raised. Her and Pete had raised Roscoe up in Stanford, but when Pete died she had to get away and went back to Harrodsburg to live. During that great snow her and Pete were snowbound without a bag of rice or a sack of corn meal to their name. But Pearline made pinto beans and light bread and they drank hot sweet tea and sang hymns when the TV wouldn't come in clear.

When her memories started reaching a painful place, Pearline snaps back to the reality: She is here in Lois and Roscoe's house.

"Hazel, will you look at that dress that woman's got on today." That's the kind of talk Hazel expects.

"Uh huh, purple for God sakes and a mite low in the front. She's trying her best to sleep with Tom." She hears the excitement in Hazel's voice.

Tom and Carol, the news anchors. Pearline and Hazel imagine their personal lives.

"Poor Wendy, with them cute little kids at home." They remember Tom's wife waving for the cameras with the kids on the Christmas special last year.

Pearline almost feels ashamed when she pictures Hazel alone in Harrodsburg in front of her small television, the kind you have to get up to change the station on. And here she was, in front of a television nearly big as the wall, Tom and Carol's faces nearly big enough to reach out and touch.

At the end of the news, Hazel grows quiet and sulky. "You coming home, Pearline?" and then, before Pearline answers, Hazel adds, "I sure hope you do."

By October, in the morning, before Roscoe scurries off to work and that woman scurries off to whatever it is that she does, Pearline lays in the bed, playing sleep. She has come to enjoy it when they come in to check on her. Roscoe wakes her up to give her her medicine and kisses her on the forehead, right between the eyes. She likes that. She's proud of him. He's a blood tester up at the hospital. They don't have that many black blood testers around here, not even over in Danville. You'd probably have to drive almost clear to Lexington to find a black blood tester but Roscoe is one right here in Stanford. Pearline loves to see him in the white uniform. He's nearly a doctor, she's convinced of that.

"Mama, you up?" he asks with the perfect bedside manner of Dr. Somebody.

"Oh, baby, I didn't hear you come in."

"Can you raise up a little and take this blood pressure pill?" Roscoe cups Pearline's back and scoots her up enough to place the pills in her mouth like she's a helpless patient.

"I need some water, don't want no orange juice this morning."

"Mama, you know you need to take it with orange juice to help your potassium along."

Potassium, Pearline thinks to herself, *what a word*? All that smarts wasted on being a blood tester. They ought to let him do some other things up at that hospital.

"My potassium's fine, son. What I need is a big glass of ice water."

Pearline likes playing this game in the mornings now. If Roscoe and Lois are going to make her old and feeble, then she will use it to her advantage. She's never been waited on so much before.

Lois breaks the solitude. "Miss Pearline," she sings coming through the door, "You look so beautiful this morning. Fresh and perky." It's like a record. Lois says the same thing every morning but Pearline knows she's being fattened for the kill. Get her healthy and send her ass back home. She can see Lois praying for the day.

"You take care of yourself today." She winks at Pearline and kisses her on the cheek, "Call me if you need me. The number's on the kitchen table.

"Bye, Honey. You are so sweet." Pearline could act too. She was Lena Horne made over.

"Bye, Sweetie," Lois says to Roscoe, gives him a kiss fit for an uncle, and is out the door.

"A good wife would have cooked you breakfast," Pearline says the minute Lois is gone.

"Mama, don't start. Lois is too busy to cook breakfast for me every morning or for herself for that matter, but she fixed breakfast for you. It's on the kitchen table waiting as usual."

"Hmmp. Poached eggs again and dry toast?" Pearline pokes her lips out like a child.

"Just what the doctor ordered. Remember?"

"How in the world would a body ever forget?"

Roscoe winks at his mother and is out the door.

"Mama, get up and move about. It's good for you," he yells from the other room.

"What's that?" Pearline asks, but she hears him just fine. She cups her mouth and giggles.

"Have a good day, Mama. Call me if you need anything."

After the house is clear, Pearline bolts from the bed. The first order of business is to take a shower. She uses Lois's smell-good bath gel and makes the bathroom smell like lilac. She slips into one of Lois's silky robes. Lois is a big woman and Pearline is thin but she likes the feel of the material against her skin. She wraps it around her body several times and ties the bow across her belly. She owns nothing like this.

She descends the basement steps and retrieves her breakfast from Roscoe's fishing tackle refrigerator. She pulls out the jowl bacon from the bottom rack. Upstairs, she slices it thin then fries up two pieces. She wraps Lois's bland eggs in newspaper and slides them into the trash, and then breaks two of her own and fries them in the remaining bacon grease. She salts the eggs from the little shaker she pulls from the pocket of the silk robe. The toast she salvages, but spreads margarine and apple butter over it. She makes herself a cup of instant coffee, heavy with cream and sugar and sits down to a real breakfast.

After breakfast, Pearline enters Lois and Roscoe's bedroom. She pulls a jogging suit from the drawer. One of Lois's, a purple one that make a swooshing noise when she walks. Pearline has grown accustomed to the plastic feel of the fabric. She slips into the pants and folds them at the waist until they fit and then secures them with a safety pin. She puts on a T-shirt and then the jacket, which hangs loosely from her shoulders. She slips into socks and then gets her own soft-soled shoes from the bedroom. Before she leaves, she dabs on a bit of lipstick and tucks her good blood pressure report down deep in her purse.

Outside, Pearline stretches her feet against the porch before she begins her walk. She ties the scarf to the back like she sees the young folks do on television. She bends her waist from side to side like the runners on CNN before a track meet.

She strikes out down Water Street, her fist at her sides, pumping back and forth with her steps. She breathes the cold air in through her nose and out her mouth. Her hips wiggle as she fast-walks. She feels her calves stretching, a slow burning in her thighs. She lifts her chin up and walks. Today she will walk further. Down past Carter's Grocery and on around by where the Greyhound bus station used to be. She feels good enough to walk to Harrodsburg. To walk right up to Hazel's house and ring the doorbell.

"Hazel," she'll say. "Come on, old girl! You got to live till you die."

Man Crazy

Mona

Man Crazy

The unseasonable warmth of winter has ended abruptly. Outside Dr. Neal's office, a stinging, cold rain has fallen. A sheet of ice is forming on the parking lot. Inside the waiting room, a sprinkling of women, their respective spouses and concerned loved ones, all sit between chairs piled with coats, jackets, purses and gloves. The walls are a sickly, green pastel and Mona sits alone. She wishes for pictures on the walls, some distraction that would rescue her from her own mind. Her brain is full.

In this room among the swelling bellies, Mona is aware of the unseen maladies swarming in the bodies of these women. Uterine cancer, tumors, yeast infections, sexually transmitted diseases—the possibilities are endless. Mona is comforted by the antiseptic smell of the waiting room.

Mona catches a glimpse of herself in the glass that boxes the doctor's staff off from the patients. She touches a stray patch of hair and notices a small, pregnant woman in the corner who appears to be a teenager. A young man with sky-blue eyes, the baby's father most likely, sits beside her. The girl looks miserable, bloated and her face is round and puffy. The baby's father has the same look on his face as the men in the mall holding purses. The young woman squirms uncomfortably in her seat as though the baby swelling inside her belly is too large for her tiny, girlish body. They are both just kids, yet innocence has left their faces with this news or perhaps with some other recent hardship. Mona wonders but only locks eyes with the boy, who is hungry for his youth. Mona can tell.

When she gives the others a last once-over, Mona is relieved that she is indeed the best-looking woman in the room. She prances across the carpet, taking the longest route, to retrieve a copy of *Cosmopolitan.* She grins at the husbands and boyfriends, sits and smoothes the creases out of her skirt. She crosses her legs and pulls the cleavage-showing purple sweater up a bit. Not lady-like to show too much. She meets the stares of the women and buries her head into the magazine. She eyes the tall, thin woman spread out before her horizontally on the page, her hand supporting her head, her one-piece fuchsia bathing suit hugging her slinky body. The blue of the ocean riding the beach behind her, even the off-white sand accentuates her features. *All make-up and airbrushing*, Mona thinks to herself. She begins to read the article about being fit for the summer.

After a few minutes, she raises her eyes above the magazine and sweeps the room again. She attempts to take inventory. Pregnant, pregnant, change of life, annual checkup, pregnant, and so forth. She decides that the solemn fiftyish woman must be awaiting news of uterine cancer or hysterectomy. Her legs are clamped shut tight; her box purse is on her lap covering the infirmity. The others, she concludes from the looks on their faces, have hormonal problems or some other pre-menopausal woes. Mona is there for her annual. She catches the young father-to-be staring at the high spot on her stocking, where the skirt meets her thigh. She smiles at him and he looks nervously away.

Mona's a strange bird for sure, forty-something, dressing like twenty—a tight, black skirt and clingy sweater. Pancake makeup hiding every blemish. Every hint of gray buried under a monthly dousing of hair dye. Sometimes black, sometimes auburn depending on her mood. Red, shiny lip-gloss and four-inch black pumps that hurt her feet. Beneath the grand facade, a bit of truth dances through her youngish bones because Mona *is* still beautiful, aging of course, but shapely and spry. She still turns heads but with the overdoing she is a spectacle for sure.

Through the blur of the photographs in the magazine she thinks of all the men she's had and her insatiable craving for more. There have been great numbers of men. Somehow, though, she rationalizes, *I loved them all, each and every one of them.* It's not anything she can explain, nothing that she can find words for. She's always needed a man but does not consider herself a whore. There's something about catching a man's eye and holding it. Mona loves the newness: the awkward fumbling of buttons, the almost touches, the wait and the yearning. What happens when they are on top of her, sweaty, thrusting and grunting is the worse part. Even as a girl she knew her own magic. She could shame a grown man, cup his eyes in her hands like water and rub them all over her face, her breasts, her hips.

In the doctor's office, she can still smell the musk of Kiki's skin.

Kiki was her first.

She can see the strong, sharp features of Isaiah.

Hear Clark's deep voice whispering in her ear on the dance floor.

Jake was the white one. Tow-headed and slim. Handsome.

Ralph was perfect at least for six months.

Marvin was the one she thought she always wanted, a businessman with gray eyes from Wytheville, Virginia.

Craig had been the first of her husbands, the father of most of her children. He had a love jones for Thelonious Monk and not a dollar to his name. A Renaissance man, a habitual entrepreneur.

Then Douglas, husband number two, who painted nude pictures of her in his studio while the children played Twister and ate pretzels in the other room.

Paul was number three. The boring one, the number cruncher who promised her a new house in one of Lexington's suburbs.

And of course there were others. Too many to recount in great detail.

And finally, Raymond, the current boyfriend, the possible fourth husband. Mature, wise; a good kisser. The kind of man who has insurance and retirement, someone you can grow old with.

Her mind sifted through them all, one by one. But love had always been the core in Mona's mind. The kind of love that kept a couple married for life. Just like those old couples she saw in church, still holding hands and kissing each other on the cheek after sixty years of marriage, exchanging glances over something cute the grandchildren did. That is what she wanted. With each of the three husbands, that's what she had hoped for. With the boyfriends, even with the ones she had just slept with. *Love*, Mona says to herself aloud and gains some stares in the waiting room.

Lying on her back underneath Kiki she felt certain this was the beginning of something. She had clenched her teeth at the pain and looked up at him. He kissed her hard and without his tongue, like she had seen on *The Doctors* and *The Days of Our Lives*. *Love*, she had thought. But it hadn't turned out that way at all. When morning came, she was just his sister's best friend again—a little girl, even though she had thought herself womanly and seductive at seventeen. Kiki was embarrassed, ashamed really, his eyes darting from the ceiling to the floor avoiding her, all of her. He was twenty-five. Mona remembered the pain and the knotted up wad of a heart she had left back then. It had shrunk to the size of a crab apple, knobby and hard. That is when she began to search. To search for something she couldn't quite name and something she hadn't quite gotten.

All she thought she ever wanted was a good man, but she loved her babies, although they were just byproducts of her search. She loved her children even more fiercely between men. It was the children who had gotten her through the hard times and the heartbreak. She held them in her lap then, and rocked the hurt away when they were little. Mona has never quite been the "mother" type. She did what she was supposed to do. She kissed and hugged them. She made sure they had new shoes and coats in August and Christmas presents in December. But she is man crazy. Her children have always been a close second to her weekend getaways in the mountains, her midnight trysts, and her honeymoons at the beach. Somehow she couldn't help herself.

The nurse calls her name and Mona stands, straightens her skirt and walks with a walk like she knows all the men in the waiting room are looking and they are. To give the father-to-be one last look, she turns and pauses as though she has forgotten something.

"How are you Mona?" the nurse asks.

"Girl, I'm doing."

"The kids?"

"Fine. The oldest is in college." Mona flips her hair and adjusts the strap of her purse on her right shoulder when she sees Dr. Neal retreating from one of the patient rooms. Dr. Neal has been her doctor forever.

The nurse shows her to the room and hands her the paper dress to change into. She folds her clothes neatly and places them in the silver metal chair. When Dr. Neal and the nurse enter the room Mona is sitting in her paper gown on the edge of the exam table trying to be dignified, her back held straight, her legs crossed as though she's wearing a taffeta ball gown. Dr. Neal takes her hand and shakes it firmly.

"Good to see you," he says. "Any problems?"

"No."

"How's the family? The kids must be grown."

"The family is good. The kids are growing like weeds," Mona answers, trying to remain as charming as she can be under the naked circumstances. She has always found what comes next humiliating.

When she is on the table, her legs wide in the stirrups and she first feels Dr. Neal's gloved finger then the plastic instrument in her insides, she is saddened.

"You'll feel a little pressure," he says.

"You're doing fine," the nurse says, and at least she knows what it's like.

Mona listens to the clicking of the instrument widening the opening of her uterus, looks at Dr. Neal, who is handsome for an elderly man and remembers the feeling after sex: an emptiness, this borderline whorish feeling like she has been pounded into submission. It's over and she mourns the loving part, the before-part, like the death of a relative. Usually there is no cuddling afterwards but sometimes the man rubs her face gently as if to say thank you. Usually he rolls away from her and sighs a fulfilled sigh and when she stares at him he says, "What?" or "Wasn't that good?" To the *What?* She answers, *Nothing*. To the: *Wasn't that good?* She nods her head, yes. It's then that the man adjusts his privates like a handshake on a job well done and smiles. Sometimes Mona nestles in the curve of the man's arm to let him know everything is fine and tries to believe it herself. But most times she's gone. In her mind she's already moved on, searching for the next man, looking for something—hoping that with him things will be different.

Before I met my Father

Angie

Before I met my Father

All the years before I met my father, he was who I needed him to be. When I was seven, maybe eight, he worked in a candy factory, and brought me as many Redhots, Now-or-Laters, Lemonheads and Laffy Taffy as I wanted. When I was ten, he made Barbie dolls. At fourteen, I said he was a roadie with the Jackson Five. But nobody in Middleburg had ever seen my father. Truth was, I had never seen him either. Didn't even know his name until I was fifteen.

In 1978, my mother and I lived with my grandparents right outside Middleburg on Route 198... My mother was trying to recover from a breakdown and any word about my father was cursed.

My mother was a true-d yo-yo. On her down days I took the long way around her chair so as not to walk in front of the TV when her stories were on. She eyed me like a bobcat, waiting for one fuck-up. I played quiet mouse, imagining myself walking on clouds or cotton balls. I fed myself, warming up a can of ravioli or beanie weenies or eating corn flakes or Vienna sausage. Careful not to clang my spoon against the bowl or to rattle the dishes into the sink until my grandmother came home. On her up days, we held hands, window shopped at the dime store over in Liberty, or jumped in my grandfather's old LTD and headed up to the farm so we could wade in the creek or swim. At home we played hopscotch and fixed fried apple pies. She kissed me on the lips like only a mother could and smiled so wide that I could have counted every single one of her teeth. My mother was pretty then, hair the color of coal that twined loop-de-loops on each side of her cheekbones. Lips thin like a white woman's. Her body long, straight and upright like a cane stalk.

My mother and grandmother floated secrets around my grandfather's head. I made myself invisible so I could know things that my grandfather didn't. He never knew about the nerve pills that hid in the bottom of my mother's brassier drawer, or about the loud cursing sessions that my mother and my grandmother had, but I did.

I was fifteen, and witnessing the end of one of these exchanges, when I heard my father's name for the first time. My grandmother, dressed in an orange, fuzzy housecoat and slippers, stood between my mother and the TV. She shook a finger in my mother's face and said, "That is why…that is exactly *why* that good-for-nothing Leonard Eldridge left you high and dry with a wet ass and a big belly."

I was bent over my homework at the kitchen table and pretended I hadn't heard a thing. I didn't dare look up, but a song was singing itself through my head. After my homework was done, after washing the supper dishes and climbing the stairs to my room, I wrote his name down before it danced away.

Leo-nard El-dridge, Leo-nard El-dridge.

I looked in the mirror.

Girl, ain't you Leonard Eldridge's daughter?

Yes, I sure am.

Thought so. You the spitting image of him.

I pushed my nose toward the mirror for a closer look. Somewhere in my reflection I could see my mother's nose and cheekbones, but I imagined my other features belonged to Leonard Eldridge. I examined myself, trying to get a glimpse of my father. I took out a piece of notebook paper and wrote his name on it and tucked it underneath my pillow, hoping that a face I could recognize would turn up in my dreams.

I sat in algebra, English and social studies, writing his name on sheets of notebook paper, on my desk, and into the palm of my hand with red ink hearts all around it. As summer approached, everything about me that had always been wilted, sprung up straight. It was the Leonard Eldridge in me working its way to the surface. Even my grandfather couldn't temper the wanting beneath my skin. Certain my family knew more about my father than they let on, I practiced sitting them down in the living room. My mother in her chair, my grandmother in the rocker, and my grandfather stretched out along the couch. I stood in front of the mirror rehearsing, saw all their mouths gaped open and heard the hush come over the room. I wrote practice notes that, once they reached perfection, would be placed on the breakfast table beneath the sugar bowl to be found and read after I was safely in school.

One morning, the week before school was out, I stood at the sink brushing my teeth. In the mirror even those parts that settled behind my teeth, under my tongue, and beyond the pink parts of my opened throat seemed to belong to my father. My grandfather had already left for the farm. My grandmother was somewhere else, already busy cleaning up white folk's houses. My mother was already up, showered and dressed, eagerly staring into the TV, and taking in whatever it provided for her. I sat at the kitchen table eating my corn flakes and writing practice notes. I wadded them up, tore them into tiny pieces and deposited them into the wastebasket that hid beneath the kitchen sink alongside the ammonia and mousetraps. At the table I tore a fresh piece of lined paper from my tablet and bore my number two pencil hard into the sheet. Each big block letter took up three lines and I wrote:

I KNOW LEONARD ELDRIDGE IS MY DADDY

AND I WANT TO SPEND THE SUMMER WITH HIM.

Short, direct—an open invitation for anyone who entered the kitchen. Throughout the day, the paper and its bold scribbles haunted me. After school I rode the bus home but didn't go inside the house. I caught a ride with Steve Wells, a white boy with a dark, green Camaro. Two strikes especially in this place where six black families were scattered throughout the county like a half dozen raisins thrown against a hillside of snow. We were at the same time invisible and seen too, too well.

"Where you headed?" I asked leaning back into the seat and looking him dead in the eye.

"Wherever you want to go." He smiled. I turned my head toward the window, tried to quell the panic rising beneath my belt buckle.

"Up on the creek, to the farm," I said trying to sound sure and confident.

"Your folks up there today?"

"No." I saw the lines in his forehead rise up in a curious fashion but I didn't let on like I noticed.

Steve's car eased onto the gravel road stirring up dust. "I'm getting my car dirty for you," he said looking over at me with a sly look. "You know there has to be a pay back."

"No, I know no such thing." I said running my hands through my hair like a white girl. I knew he would like that.

When we reached a part of the farm that I was most familiar with we got out of the car. I looked up at Steve and he seemed taller than I remembered from English class. His shoulders seemed wider. Cute, too. He stood over me cock-legged, his legs outside mine. Me leaning back against the hood of the car. His hair splayed out by the wind like yellow wings.

"Now what?" he said drawing his face closer to mine.

"Now, nothing," I said moving out of his grasp.

The trees had just begun to sprout bits of green and the fields along the creek bank were still covered with vibrant pink, blue and white wild flowers. The air was fresh and clean and I could see my grandfather's barn in the distance. I tried to picture my grandfather at home, gathering the women around him to discuss my Leonard

Eldridge note but I let that thought float out with the wind that rode in and out of Steve's hair.

I slid down the bank, jumped the smaller part of the stream, ran across the gravel and ducked under the bridge before Steve caught up. When he slid down the embankment and came to a stop, I was already nestled into a nook, a spot just large enough for two people to fit into. He scooted in beside me, his hip jutting into mine. I hit him square in the shoulder and pushed him so hard he nearly fell in the creek. We both laughed.

"So what the hell?" Steve said regaining his balance and moving in so close I felt uncomfortable again. "Why'd you want to come way out here?"

"Needed time to think." I left it at that.

Steve's daddy was always two-sheets-in-the-wind. His mother scared of almost everything, especially his daddy. His sister, who was two years younger than me, was pregnant by some grease monkey over in Dunnville. Steve had bought his car with his own money, working weekends with his Uncle Jessie. I guess I would have known everything there was to know about him if I hadn't stolen his breath. I grabbed his face at the cheeks and just as our lips met, I noticed how white his face was, white as clouds, against my hands, brown as caramel sauce. I had never kissed a boy before but I opened my lips up to the size of a lemon, like the women on my mother's stories. Steve darted his tongue in and out of my mouth and his hands wandered over me. I couldn't stop him. Didn't try. When I was sweetly exhausted just from his touch, he buttoned my blouse, buckled my jeans and said, "Let me get you home." We stood up and hugged. I felt him hard down there on my leg.

In the car I was silent, my head still swimming, wishing this were a story that I could tell somebody. Sometimes in summer, I shared secrets with my cousin, Junior, when I visited them in Stanford but this was a story that I couldn't even tell him. A story that I had to keep to myself.

Back in town, Steve pulled his car onto Route 198 but I convinced him to let me out a long ways from the house. He pulled my face to him and livened my mouth with his tongue again.

"Gonna see you again?" he asked. Outside the car, I looked around to see if anyone was looking and I leaned into the car to kiss him one more time.

"Maybe," I said. Nervous. I felt his corn-silk hair brush against my fingers when I pulled myself away and he was gone.

The night felt more like late fall than the beginning of summer and I walked with my arms crossed toward home. A blue and white pick-up truck slowed beside me.

"I always wanted some nigger pussy," one of boys inside yelled, poking his red head out the window. I recognized him. John Grider from school.

"Whoo-hoo," another boy yelled from the truck.

"Let's get us some black tail," said a third voice whose face hid in the shadows.

The truck stopped and I heard a door open. I ran, flying through yards and across fences. Far behind me I heard laughing and the truck driving off in the opposite direction. I stopped to straighten my hair and pushed my shirt firmly back into my jeans. Through the front bay window of our house, I saw my family gathered in the living room, in their favorite evening positions, the white glare of the TV causing them to look like cartoons. Before I got a chance to turn the knob, I heard footsteps moving toward the direction of the door. My mother and my grandmother reacted at first in a way that I had not expected, smothering me with "worried to death." I could see my grandfather on the couch, through the arms and shoulders that fussed over me, rubbing his bent-down graying head. In the kitchen, dinner was still laid out. Chicken and dumplings, roasted potatoes, carrots and peas. Cornbread. More fried apple pies. As I settled into the seat, my grandmother placed her hands on her hips.

"Girl, where in the hell have you been?"

"Just out thinking," I said my eyes down into the plate. I raised up long enough to drain the glass of grape Kool-Aid and accidentally brought it down too hard on the table.

"Just out thinking?" my mother said making that hissing noise through her teeth, "I'm a give you something to think about."

My face was still stinging with the imprint of my mother's hand when my grandfather appeared at the kitchen doorway.

"The child wants to see her daddy. Send her and leave her be. Call up to Cincinnati and tell Leonard Eldridge his child's coming." My grandfather's voice was strong and shattering. Sent echoes, I was sure, of my father's name up and down the road. My mother's face contorted like she felt a pain somewhere and my grandmother commenced to washing dishes and tried to hum my father's name out of her house.

When I went to bed they were whisper cursing in a corner of the kitchen out of earshot like two teenage girls. But it stuck, Leonard Eldridge's name, stuck like glue in the air filling up every empty space from the cellar to the attic.

That night I fell asleep, tasting my father's name on my tongue but I dreamed of Steve Wells all night long, his corn-silk hair flapping in the wind like a bird, and me spent and quivering beneath his white hands.

Before I left for Cincinnati, Steve picked me up after school for five days straight. "Been thinking," is all I said when I got home later and somehow that was the only excuse I needed. Nobody questioned me anymore, as though discovering my father warranted some reflection. As though we had all waited all my life for this. On that fifth day, as I lay gathering my breath, Steve unzipped his pants and pulled out his thing. My grandmother would have said penis. It looked ugly in Steve's hand. Red. Veined. Throbbing. Not what I expected.

"You still a virgin, ain't you?" he asked rubbing his hand back and forth.

"Yes," I tried to say with some confidence but it came out a low-pitched squeal. Steve turned his back to me but I could see. The wind caught his hair and he appeared to be about to take flight. His breath sped up and finally when it returned to calm he turned back around, zipped his pants and held me close.

In bed the night before I left, I thought of my father. Tried to picture his wife, Terri, and the boys Mama called 'the stepbrothers.' I wondered what Cincinnati was like. But mostly I thought of Steve Wells. It was a warm night and through my open window I smelled the freshness of new, cut grass and listened to the crickets and the katydids. I snuggled down into the covers of my bed like it was the very last night in the world that I would be nesting there.

At the Greyhound bus station in Stanford, my mother and my grandmother fumed over me, snapping the red windbreaker I was wearing right up to my chin.

"You call if them people don't treat you right," my grandmother said pressing two twenties into the center of my hand. "You come home early if you want to."

She kissed my cheek leaving it wet. I felt it glistening in the morning sun but I didn't wipe it off. My mother hugged me tight and said, "Have fun and you call as soon as you get there. Call collect if you have to."

She pushed me away from her but held me at the shoulders to get a final look. Then pulled me into her once more.

"You look just like that damn man," she said, "your damned old daddy," this time smiling. My grandfather hugged me too.

"Be good," was all he said but I seen more hiding behind the thicket of his eyebrows.

"Bye. Love y'all," I said over my shoulder as I boarded the bus. The bus driver, red and burley, tipped his hat toward me as he took my ticket.

"Cincinnati?"

I nodded, yes, and scooted into an empty seat. I could feel flocks of butterflies easing into my gut before the bus reached the Danville stop in the next small town. The Greyhound bus smelled like piss. People everywhere. Crammed in like jigsaw puzzle pieces. A black-haired woman sat across from me with a little black-haired boy. The boy jumped and darted toward the window. Toward the isle. She made it her job for all the hours we were together to jerk and swat the child, who was a smaller version of her. She swatted his arms, his thighs. I guessed him to be four or five. Behind me there was a black man. He reminded me of Mr. Hershel from church, because I saw a piece of home in him somewhere. I wanted to talk to him, but he ignored me and never even looked my way. A couple of brown-headed kids who looked as if they were on a honeymoon. A girl, much younger than me, traveling alone, her copy of her ticket, her name, *B-e-c-k-y*, in big red letters attached with a purple diaper pin to her blouse. She smiled at me when she was not sleeping. In Lexington, I changed buses. Again, there were no familiar faces among the many who climbed aboard the Cincinnati bus, but there were more black people. There was a family. A girl about my age, a mother, a father, and a little girl who appeared to be in her terrible twos. She was dressed in bright yellow and looked like a buttercup. The girl my age smiled. The mother nodded, hello, but nobody spoke. Across the seat from me, a couple in love. They kissed and giggled from Lexington to Cincinnati. The man, brown-skinned and dressed to the nines, kept one hand around the woman's shoulders like she was something too good to let go of. She was birdlike and light-skinned. Something shy-looking about her good looks. Her hair swept up in some magnificent bun snaking along the back of her head. Her lips painted pumpkin between the times that the man kissed it away. Every time he kissed the pumpkin rouge from her lips, she replaced it from the tube she pulled from the small pocketbook that rested in her lap like a kitten. I watched them and tried to picture my mother with my father like this, in love and running off.

When we arrived in Cincinnati, there was a whole forest of black men inside the bus station. Each time one came close or nodded or said, "hi," my heart beat a little faster. The tall, skinny, dark-skinned one with bell-bottom blue jeans. No. The short, light-skinned man with alligator boots. No. Seersucker pants. No. Hat tilted to the right. No. Freckles. No. Loud booming laugh. No. The fatherly looking man carrying a bouquet of flowers. No.

Finally, a dark-brown man in blue work pants and a matching shirt approached me—he had "Leonard" beamed in white script type across one shirt pocket. Norwood Plumbing on the other pocket. Not tall, not short. Not handsome, not ugly. An Afro. An Afro, a pick stuck in the side. A small mustache. Nothing special. Nothing grand.

"Baby Girl?" he said. His arms stretched out, lean and bony like tree limbs and scooped me up off the floor. He smelled of sweat and some spicy, sweet cologne. A smell I liked.

"Hi," I managed, not able to think of anything else.

He winked and smiled at me. "Dead on your mama," he said looking me up and down, searching for something familiar. I surveyed his face; yet saw only a hint of me inside, beneath the eyes I thought.

Leonard Eldridge's house was larger than I expected it to be. Red brick with a wrap-around screened porch. Inside everything was some shade of blue and most of it brand new. It smelled like I thought the ocean would. A feel-good smell. Spotless. Thick shag carpet. Navy blue couch and matching chair. Walls the color of the sky on a cloudless day. I had never seen anything like it. The three other members of my father's family entered the room. All from separate directions. Terri, my father's wife, hugged me so tight that I felt I would suffocate in her large breasts. She was dark, with hips that spread out like two perfect cantaloupe on each side of her body. Dressed in tight jeans and a body suit, she looked like something about to pop open. I immediately wondered what my father saw in her that he had not been able to find somewhere in my mother's willowy frame.

"Look at you," she said, "Leonard Eldridge made over." And I giggled embarrassingly loud at yet another interpretation of who I was. The boys and my father looked like triplets. Leonard Jr. was fourteen, only one year younger than me and Antwan was ten. They were dressed alike in green Lacoste shirts and matching plaid, green and white shorts. Their dark faces cleaned and lotioned. Right away I felt jealous that Junior carried my father's name. I had been his first-born child. I pondered the names Leona, Leontyne, Leonora, Leonard Etta—replacing each of them with my own.

There was an uncomfortable quiet in the living room, all of us standing and looking at each other until my father said, "Boys, show your sister around." Antwan grabbed my suitcase with a determination that only ten-year-old boys possess.

"What you got in this thing?" he asked halfway up the steps. "Rocks?"

Junior just marched forward like a soldier carrying out his father's orders. At the top of the steps Antwan let my suitcase thud in the hallway.

"Bathroom, my room, Antwan's."

Junior carried on, yelled out the rooms like the red, burly Greyhound bus driver, only stone-faced. At Antwan's room, the ten-year-old waved his hands out like a circus ringmaster.

"Ta-Da," he said.

"Dumb," Junior said and pushed him down to the floor. I laughed.

"Mama and Daddy's room, kitchen, den."

The upstairs bathroom was zebra. Black and white tile. Rug. Shower curtain. Waste basket. Complete with ceramic zebras resting on the back of the toilet. Junior's room was sports. Basketball. Baseball. Football. A large orange basketball net was painted on his wall. A ball being released from large black hands into its open mouth. Antwan's room was cartoons. Fat Albert. Pink Panther. Bugs. Tweety. The room where my father and his wife slept was somewhere between black pride and Africa. Busts of black women with large hoop earrings and large Afros were on the nightstand. African masks on the walls. Leopard skin rugs, bedspread and curtains. Green vines snaking around the walls. Black panthers and lions that glowed under a blue-black light. The room they called mine looked like the sun. Yellow and orange. Even the small bathroom attached was yellow and orange. Tangerines, lemons and limes painted on the walls.

Terri served lasagna, salad and breadsticks for dinner. Not what I was used to but I liked it.

"I want to spend some time with you tomorrow, Baby Girl," my father said. "It's been a long time."

I just nodded. Junior rolled his eyes, Antwan giggled, and Terri smiled so wide I thought her face would burst. I stared at my father between bites, trying to find something more than ordinary that would make him the father I had imagined all these years, but I couldn't find a thing.

Later that night, in the room the color of the sun, I wrote to my family:

I am enjoying my vacation. My daddy lives in a big house.

They are very nice people.

To Steve I wrote: *I am bored and would much rather be home with you*...and signed it Love, Leona—just for fun. I tossed and turned all night, dreaming of my mother and father. They were the couple on the bus. Leonard Eldridge was unable to keep his hands off her. They were so much in love. Their lips pressed together every chance they got.

My father took me to the King's Island amusement park, the Cincinnati Zoo, and to all his favorite restaurants. He held my hand like I was a little child and stared at me for minutes at a time. He asked me about school. Boyfriends. Interests and hobbies. I felt like I was being interviewed for a beauty pageant or a news show. I gave him generic answers and kept my disappointment in him suppressed.

"What happened?" I finally asked him during one of these outings. "What happened between you and Mama?" I asked again when he looked at me as though he had misunderstood.

"Baby Girl," he said after a long pause. Then he cleared his throat. "Sometimes..."

"What happened?" I repeated.

"I just didn't love her," he said, his head hanging down to his chest. "She was a nice girl," he said and finally, "She told me she couldn't get pregnant."

Fifteen years and it had all boiled down to nothing. My father hadn't been madly in love with my mother at all. Leonard Eldridge looked me in the face, then looked away—like he feared what he saw there.

"That don't mean I don't love you, Baby Girl," he said. On the family outings I felt like an outsider, a long lost cousin maybe, but never like a daughter. There was always some inside family joke that I didn't get.

"Remember when we was at Disney World," Antwan said one night.

"No, I don't remember. I've never been to Disney World in my life," I said and went to the yellow and orange room and locked the door.

One Sunday when we were at a restaurant, me, Junior and Antwan were eating ice cream. Somehow we had all chosen chocolate. Our father must have seen a flash of a family portrait in us.

"Look at y'all," he said, "been eating chocolate ice cream since y'all was little things. Since before y'all could walk," he added.

"You don't know a damn thing about me," I said and went outside and sat on the hood of my father's car until they were ready to leave. It was the first time I had ever cursed in front of adults.

I went home a week early. At the Greyhound bus station, my father hugged me but my arms wouldn't move to hug him back.

"Come back and see me, Baby Girl," he said his voice cracking like an egg.

I stepped on the bus refusing to satisfy him with a good bye or a look back.

I returned home with a sharper tongue and rougher edges. I clanged the dishes in the sink and walked in front of my mother's TV stories, daring a response. Wanting her to cross me. I was armed and ready and she knew it. I came home to find Steve riding a blonde girl around in his car. They could have passed for twins. Both tow-headed and skin so white. One evening, when the sun was turning the color of my room back in Cincinnati, I was walking home from the store. Steve pulled up beside me.

"I'm sorry," he said. "I miss you, need a ride?"

"Go to hell you white yellah-haired bastard," I screamed and he drove off, his tires leaving a long black snake streak across the pavement.

Every night I cried myself to sleep and woke up more salty than the day before. I refused to talk to Leonard Eldridge when he called. I wanted my real father back. The one I had gotten used to not knowing.

On Thanksgiving break, Mr. Hershel's nephew, Stewart, came to spend the week with him. He was from Tennessee. Just in town while his mother, Mr. Hershel's sister, had her gall bladder out. I summed him up in church. Dark-skin. Smooth as slate rock. Tall. Eyes like almonds. Hands big as dinner plates. My grandmother invited him and Mr. Hershel to our house for Sunday supper. After supper, outside on the porch, Stewart said, "What do y'all do way down here? I'd be bored shitless."

"I'll show you," I said jingling the keys to my grandfather's LTD.

I took Stewart along the back roads to the farm up on the creek, dust blowing behind us like a tornado. Underneath the bridge, he kissed me softly, so soft I could barely feel his lips. A kiss like my mother's, closed lipped and sweet. I felt him shudder when I pried his lips apart with my tongue. I unzipped my jacket, unbuttoned my blouse, and let him touch me anywhere he wanted to.

He stammered something, words I couldn't make out, his breath wild. When I took out his thing and pressed it against me he hesitated.

"Don't worry. It's okay," I whispered.

What I remember most is the quiet of Stewart's breath rising to a loud moan, his body drawn up tight as a fist, entering me like a weapon. I could feel the father I had always known being buried so deep that I was sure no parts of him remained in my reflection. He was lost and I would never be able to stretch my fingers long enough or far enough to pull him back.

Afterword

Marianne Worthington

Crystal Wilkinson was an important debut artist for the young Toby Press, founded in 1999, when *Water Street* first appeared in 2002 (second printing in 2005). Toby Press had published her first collection, *Blackberries, Blackberries*, just two years prior. *Water Street* was a finalist for the Orange Prize for Fiction (the United Kingdom's most prestigious international literary prize) and for the Hurston/Wright Legacy Award. The opening story in *Water Street,* "My Girl Mona," won the *Indiana Review* Fiction Prize. Now with this new reprint of *Water Street* readers can revisit and reclaim the community of vibrant storytellers Wilkinson created in this story sequence. With the publication of Wilkinson's acclaimed and long-awaited new novel, *The Birds of Opulence,* in 2016, readers can further enjoy the continuation and opening of stories from some of the characters who first spoke to us in *Water Street.*

In the prologue story, "Welcome to Water Street," the narrator says, "On Water Street, every person has at least two stories to tell. One story that the light of day shines on; the other that lives only in the pitch black of night, the kind of story carried beneath the breastbone, near the heart, for safekeeping." These are the last lines of "Welcome to Water Street," a communal credo, spoken collectively by the residents of Water Street as an affirmation of faith, of fact, of myth. The story serves as both welcome and primer to the larger collection of Wilkinson's linked stories. This narrator is much like a community choir, singing confidently of the world we are about to enter and helping us understand how to enter that world. We should be holding hands, for this is a book of confessions spoken by people who are self-aware yet haunted. Their story is lyrical and fierce: "We love being close to the people we've known since we entered the world," they profess. "And we hate it. Everybody knows your name here. Everyone has committed the long lists of your kin to memory." When we finish "Welcome to Water Street" we have been schooled: we have a set of directions and opinions on the bloodlines, economic status, community traditions, cultural heritage, and geography of the stories we will be entering.

Water Street is a book of stories that is latched together not only by community and family and geography but also by narrative impulse. The stories in *Water Street* are mostly first-person accounts told by African American people (with one exception) living together in a narrow geographical area in central Kentucky. *Water Street* is a story cycle about how we tell our stories and why. It is decisively a metastory, a book about storytelling, and we realize it almost instinctually and instantly as we witness Yolanda talking in the opening story, "My Girl Mona."

Yolanda is telling her friend Mona the stories related to her panic attacks and then telling her doctor about telling those stories to Mona. And Yolanda isn't even talking to her doctor while she tells her story. She is talking to *us,* the readers. This layering of story upon story is a much more complicated yet entertaining type of storytelling. We become nosy readers. We enjoy listening to Yolanda not only re-create her stories but also recount in great detail how she *told* those stories to Mona and to her doctor. "I know she can't wait for me to hush," Yolanda tells her doctor, "but I keep on talking like my life depends on it." Then, shortly after, she says, "I stop talking for just a second before I start back up, timing it just right, making sure it's not long enough for her to jump in." Later, she tells readers that she is aware of us after she uses the word "ass" and then says, "I should have said 'hind end' in front of Doctor but I didn't. I was comfortable, like we were old friends." For Yolanda, storytelling is a source of power while also serving as a form of salvation for her troubles. Yolanda is probably suffering from bipolar disorder (we learn that later when her brother tells his story), and she is using storytelling as a way to steady herself and her chaotic surroundings. Ultimately, Yolanda is, like the rest of the speakers in *Water Street,* carrying her stories out of the "pitch black of night," out from "beneath the breastbone" and into *our* hearts, "for safekeeping."

Yolanda's family and neighbors, one by one, tell us their stories, too—her husband Junior, her brother KiKi, her friend Mona, her neighbors Mouse, Sandy, and Toni, and others. As each new story is told we learn more and more about the people who live on Water Street (and beyond). These people recur in each other's stories, so the connections and themes deepen and resonate as each teller faces the reader squarely and speaks with conviction. The tales told in *Water Street* build a larger cultural *biomythography,* a term used by Audre Lorde in describing her 1982 autobiography, *Zami: A New Spelling of My Name,* and defined as combining elements of history, biography, and myth, a type of story built from many sources.

This Audre Lorde connection seems important to make since Wilkinson considers Lorde a spiritual guide and a literary ancestor. She said recently, "I have looked to Audre Lorde for guidance as a black woman for a long time." Wilkinson designs creative writing classes for her students in biomythography and has studied Lorde's work as teacher and as storyteller to fashion her own teaching and writing. And we see this influence in *Water Street* as well. The stories are molded from local and private histories as each speaker builds a personal narrative and mythology of time and place. Beyond that, we understand that Wilkinson is the guiding hand behind these stories, having spent every summer of her childhood in Stanford, where she still has many family members. *Water Street* is a compelling model of how a storyteller combines personal history, biography, and myth to capture the cyclical spirit of a real place and, thus, capture the interest of her readers.

In her 1978 speech "The Use of the Erotic: The Erotic as Power," Audre Lorde asserted that the bridge between the spiritual and the political is the erotic, which Lorde defined in the speech as "those physical, emotional, and psychic expressions of what is deepest and strongest and richest within each of us." The deepest and strongest and richest expressions in the linked stories of *Water Street* are these personal and cultural histories from a primarily black community. These chronicles circle around several narrative consistencies including interracial tensions, the naming of people and places with intention (Lancaster, Liberty, Hustonville, Danville, Crab Orchard—real places, all), the cultural and interpersonal effects of learning via television and popular culture in the decade of the 1970s, the thrills and consequences of sexual awakening and expression, and ultimately the significance of telling stories. Here are just a few examples of these unifying story structures:

Junior's story, "Water Street, 1979," is a fine instance of illustrating racial inequalities and uncertainties in Stanford, Kentucky. Junior explains that his father spoke to him many times "about the birds, the bees and the white folks. . . . All the blacks lived at one end of Water Street above the hill, all the whites lived on the other end." Yet it is Junior's father who is first to organize help for the white MacIntosh family members, who have to abandon their home during a spring flood. They store their belongings in Junior's family garage, and Junior looks through the MacIntosh family photos: "I was surprised that the MacIntosh family photographs were similar to ours. Yellowed pictures of men dirtied with work, fresh from the tobacco fields. . . . I sifted through the MacIntosh children's school photographs. Frozen poses that could have been Peanut's or mine. Any of us. I left those pictures in the garage but carried their impressions to bed with me that night." Junior struggles with his responsibilities as a schoolteacher, one of the first black teachers in the county. He says, "I see the black and the brown kids get slighted by white teachers all the time. It's hard for me sometimes to keep speaking to my colleagues when I know what goes on in their classrooms." And Junior processes his feelings while remembering his sexual encounter with Bonnie (a white woman): "The guilt of messing around on my wife would come later. Seemed like a part of me was prepared for the door to be broken down by a lynch mob. Another part of me felt like I had turned my back on my mother, Yolanda and every black woman I had ever known." Junior contemplates aloud, and we contemplate with him. He is meditating on guilt, on disparity, on insecurity, and we meditate with him.

In "Sixteen Confessions of Lois Carter" we witness similar meditations, but they are spoken by the only white narrator in *Water Street.* Lois married Roscoe Givens, a black man, and her lifelong tensions between her white family of origin and her black in-laws are the subject of her narrative "confessions." Lois grew up with parents who referred to the African American children in Stanford as "little darkies" and "niggras." Her mother-in-law, Pearline, is civil on the surface, but Lois says: "I can see it in her eyes that she wishes her son had married a black woman." Lois confesses: "I live one life over there, one over here. I live my life straddled. Never standing too straight or tall in either world. The two hardly ever mix." When Pearline tells her story ("Respite") she refers to her daughter-in-law not by name but as "that woman" and discredits Lois's domestic and parenting skills. Pearline says Lois's children and grandchildren (Pearline's own grandchildren and great-grandchildren) are "like wild cats. No home training whatsoever."

Jeanette's story, "In Plain Sight," references television and popular culture as learning tools and anchor points in her development. After her father dies and her mother slips into insanity, Jeanette is sent to live with a family friend, Bertha Watkins. "When I look at her," Jeanette remarks knowingly, "she reminds me of Diahann Carroll playing Julia on TV, only Miss Watkins is a Diahann Carroll with more soul." While she watches Bertha entertain a male visitor one night, Bertha becomes "Diana Ross waiting for Billy D's kiss in *Mahogany.*" Jeanette longs for a stable family, "all happy like those smiling television shows that captured my attention on Friday nights." Other speakers from other stories also bring popular culture references to their tales (magazines, soap operas, sitcoms, movies, and songs). These cultural markers do more than give us a time frame for the stories; they reinforce the often controlled, unrealistic national narratives we are fed through mass media, which would be especially crippling for black adolescents in 1970s Kentucky.

What is most realistic in these narratives, however, are the often brutal, awkward, and painful sexual encounters the storytellers relate to us. Nearly every speaker in this story cycle has something to say about his or her sexual awakening, and it is almost never sensuous or pretty. Reverend Townsend, a Stanford minister and community worker, is ignorant of women and spends much of his energy repressing his sexual feelings for a particular woman. The Reverend learned early on from his brother that women "were there to cook and clean and to have sex with, because that was what they were good for . . . that women had a place in the world, a tiny place, like a pocket where you kept them held hostage until you needed them for something useful." On the other hand, speakers like Angie and Mona are openly sexual, but engaged in using sex in destructive ways, either as a weapon or as an antidote for loneliness, abuse, abandonment. Mona, in particular, derives no joy from sex, even though it is all she thinks about. Mona "thinks of all the men she's had and her insatiable craving for more," of her continual "search for something she couldn't quite name and something she hadn't quite gotten." She tells us of her dreaded feelings after each sexual encounter: "an emptiness, this borderline whorish feeling."

In addition to these vital narrative motifs, we can experience the stories in *Water Street* on the deepest level because the author calls us to be participant readers in the prologue story. The very definition of a short-story cycle requires that readers make the connections between the stories, thus enriching their own experiences. Our lives often operate in much the same way as a set of stories—in fragments or in seemingly unrelated hops and jumps—but we can instantly feel an organic connection to the structure of this book because we tend to right our own disparate lives through recurring memory and through storytelling. This type of involved reading experience quickens the readers' place in the telling of these stories, and that is the gift of this book. We ponder and assess our own lives through the experience of reading, and this is how Wilkinson achieves presenting a spiritual book of stories that makes political statements about race, class, gender, mental illness, and interpersonal relationships. For Crystal Wilkinson, and for the tellers of these tales, storytelling is the erotic act.

Acknowledgments

I am grateful to The Mary Anderson Center and The Hopscotch House for providing me with a quiet space to create. A special thanks to Marie Brown for her undying encouragement from the very beginning; Marita Golden and the Hurston/Wright Foundation; the Carnegie Center, especially Jan Isenhour for reading the manuscript; the Affrilachian Poets; Matthew Miller, who believes I can write; Aloma Halter, my editor, who broadened my sense of the world; and Sena Jeter Naslund, Karen Mann, Melissa Pritchard and the Spalding University family. Finally, a heartfelt thanks to Steve Snow for a renewed friendship that has tapped a spring of memories.

About the Author

Photo by Ronald Davis

Crystal Wilkinson is the author of *The Birds of Opulence*, winner of the 2016 Ernest J. Gaines Award for Literary Excellence, *Blackberries, Blackberries*, winner of the Chaffin Award for Appalachian Literature, and *Water Street*, a finalist for both the United Kingdom's Orange Prize for Fiction and the Hurston/Wright Legacy Award. Winner of the 2008 Denny Plattner Award in Poetry from *Appalachian Heritage* magazine and the Sallie Bingham Award from the Kentucky Foundation for Women, she serves as Appalachian Writer-in-Residence at Berea College and teaches in Spalding University's low residency MFA in Writing Program. She and her partner, the poet and artist Ronald Davis, own Wild Fig Books and Coffee in Lexington, Kentucky.

Kentucky Voices

Miss America Kissed Caleb: Stories
Billy C. Clark

New Covenant Bound
T. Crunk

Next Door to the Dead: Poems
Kathleen Driskell

The Total Light Process: New and Selected Poems
James Baker Hall

Driving with the Dead: Poems
Jane Hicks

Upheaval: Stories
Chris Holbrook

Appalachian Elegy: Poetry and Place
bell hooks

Crossing the River: A Novel
Fenton Johnson

The Man Who Loved Birds: A Novel
Fenton Johnson

Scissors, Paper, Rock: A Novel
Fenton Johnson

Many-Storied House: Poems
George Ella Lyon

With a Hammer for My Heart: A Novel
George Ella Lyon

Famous People I Have Known
Ed McClanahan

The Land We Dreamed: Poems
Joe Survant

Sue Mundy: A Novel of the Civil War
Richard Taylor

At The Breakers: A Novel
Mary Ann Taylor-Hall

Come and Go, Molly Snow: A Novel
Mary Ann Taylor-Hall

Nothing Like an Ocean: Stories
Jim Tomlinson

Buffalo Dance: The Journey of York
Frank X Walker

When Winter Come: The Ascension of York
Frank X Walker

The Cave
Robert Penn Warren

The Birds of Opulence
Crystal Wilkinson

Blackberries, Blackberries
Crystal Wilkinson

Water Street
Crystal Wilkinson

CPSIA information can be obtained
at www.ICGtesting.com
Printed in the USA
LVOW08s1757260517
535980LV00002B/422/P

9 780813 169101